# Charlie Says

First published in Great Britain in 2024 by Black Shuck Books

Cover design by WHITEspace

Set in Caslon by WHITEspace
www.white-space.uk

978-1-913038-89-2

*Thanks for all your support, John*

*Neil*

# Charlie Says

### by
### Neil Williamson

## BLACK
## SHUCK
## BOOKS

# Just Like That, No One's Laughing

Charlie dries right up. Blinks through the purple-green LED glare at the blank faces crowding this Edinburgh pub. They blink back, and the moment stretches. Someone coughs. Someone sniggers and, once it's begun, the laughter ripples around the space, spreading like an infection. They're all so young. Most, here for the Twitch star headliner, haven't a clue who this old guy on stage is. Let's face it, he's opening at the Fringe for a seventeen-year-old who might have a million followers but has never so much as faced an actual live audience before.

And it's a bucket show. This isn't a comeback. It's a humiliation.

Charlie has been here before, though. The stage is still his for the next twenty minutes. He needs to power through, get them back on side.

He licks his dry lips, takes a sip of his beer, winces. "Fuck's sake." As the words boom out of the speakers, he scowls at the bottle, baffled at the tropical flavours. "This isn't beer. It's mildly boozy Um Bongo."

As desperate ad libs go it's not terrible, but unsurprisingly the reference to a juice drink consigned to the packed lunches of the last century fails to land with the Gen Zers. It doesn't matter. He can use it to jump into his solid bit on the gleeful jollity that was British TV racism in the seventies and eighties. And there's nothing the current generation likes more than laughing at the shiteness of the previous one, right?

"Do the voice."

The heckle throws him all over again. He used to have a hundred put-downs in his back pocket, but now all he manages is, "You what?"

"Do the voice."

Peering into the dazzle, he's unable to identify the speaker, but it's obvious his biggest fear has been realised. There's a fan from the old days in.

"That's ancient material, mate," he says. "Well past its sell-by. This show's all about the new stuff."

"Do the Cat, you prick. Do the fucking voice!"

"Yeah, do the voice," shouts one of the young ones at the front. Her sort are ten-a-penny at the Fringe: Home Counties accent, hair twisted up in kooky knots and enough make-up and glitter to advertise to all and sundry that mummy's little performer is in a show too. She won't have paid for her ticket, but you can bet your arse she'll be outside handing out flyers later. Right now, though, she's after fun and senses there's some to be had here. "Do the voice!" she shouts again, turning it into a chant that is quickly picked up by the rest of the crowd.

There's no way Charlie's finishing his prepared set now. It's either walk off, or...

The noise comes out of him like something that has been imprisoned for decades. A foul genie in a bottle manifesting as a strangled, snarky caterwaul. When it comes to an end he tilts his head, as if listening. The way he always used to.

"What's he say?" shouts the voice from the back.

"What's he say?" Charlie repeats into the mic. He shouldn't be doing this...*mustn't*, but he can't seem to help himself. "What does Cat say?"

The ancient joke feels natural. Comfy as old steel-toed boots.

———

### The Cat's Bollocks: Pia Ward interviews Charlie Mason, Snigger.com 15/11/2013

*PW: There's been something of a Twitter storm following the announcement of this year's* I'm A Celebrity *line-up.*
*CM: I'm not really into all that social media stuff, mate.*
*PW: The petition to have you removed from the show has topped 100k and is growing by the day. You're not denying that's you in those videos?*
*CM: No, but it was a long, long time ago. People change, and I'm going into the jungle to show everyone exactly how much.*
*PW: So viewers can rest assured there won't be any unplanned appearances by the Cat?*
*CM: Not unless I'm going to have to eat his bollocks in a Bushtucker Trial. Hey, you can tell the producers I'll gladly do that if it means getting rid of that bastard once and for all.*

———

"What the ever-living fuck was that?"

Raisa Tariq pushes through the blackout curtain that marks this part of the snug off as the 'Artists' Area' and assumes the belligerent stance that has defeated many better men than Charlie. She's not a large woman and power suits have long since been consigned to the fashion trash fire that was the nineties, but you know instantly from the pose, the glare, the intemperate ripple of the perfect nails on the sleeve of her couture jacket, crimson on crimson, that she is not someone you want to piss off. The three gay Irish improvs who have been arguing over their running order for the last twenty minutes while Charlie has been necking his way with solid determination through a quarter bottle of Bells stare at the newcomer in stunned silence. Raisa cantilevers an eyebrow and they catch up with the script, taking their banal, creative discourse outside.

Raisa's rightly furious and Charlie knows he's going to have to apologise, but he's too sickened by himself to initiate it. "Nice of you to show up," he mumbles, grimacing at an awful taste that's only partly down to the whisky.

"I was still your manager last time I checked," she says through a razor-cut smile. "Showing up kinda goes with the job."

Charlie rolls his eyes in the direction of the stage, where the Twitch teen can be heard rattling breathlessly through a set that seems to consist of little more than ripping the mick out of well-known Influencers, none of whom Charlie has heard of. There might be impressions, he's not sure. They all have that weird, transatlantic, Only-Way-Is-Valley-Girl accent now, don't they? She's had a few proper laughs, though, to be fair.

"Yeah, well," he says. "Shouldn't you be out there supporting the new generation?"

Raisa comes over to perch on the arm of the dilapidated green leather couch. "Yes, I should but, despite the fact that the previous act cleared the *entire room* with his antiquated, racist bullshit – you know I couldn't actually tell you the last time I heard *Paki* used in anger on stage – young Aisha seems to be holding her own out there." Her voice is gentler, but her touch on his arm still scalds. "Charlie…?"

Charlie focuses on the label of the bottle. "*I know. I'm sorry.*" He sloshes the Scotch around. "Honestly? I can't even explain what happened out there…" Of course, he *could* explain, though he doesn't need to. They both know what it's like when your act is bombing, how you'll say almost anything to get just one laugh. Especially when the bastards goad you into it.

No, even that's not true.

Not goad. Not provoke.

*Give permission.*

Raisa extracts the whisky from his fingers and takes a long slug before handing it back. "All right. Forget about it. Start fresh tomorrow night."

"Tomorrow night?" He scoffs to cover his embarrassment at this unearned generosity. "Fuck that. There's no point in going on tomorrow night."

"Course there is, bab." When Raisa damps down the fire, her native Brummie warmth kindles her vowels. "What's our motto? This is the gig…?"

Charlie sighs, then completes the mantra they'd coined to get them through some of the more hellish performing situations they'd found themselves having to deal with over the course of their long association. "We take the cash and get the job done like fucking professionals."

"Right. Anyway, your *Modern Britain* material really is good. I wouldn't have wasted my energy convincing you to take this slot if it wasn't. It has genuine depth and perspective; coming as it does from someone who made it through the last fifty years of execrable public values…including, as your little lapse unfortunately just proved, as one of the worst offenders. The Yaxley-Lennon vs Derek Griffiths song is proper brilliant. Take it from one who knows."

"Except I've already fucked it, haven't I?" he says. "One nudge and I'm back to *enfant terrible* all over again. Worse than that. A *hasbeen terrible*. An old dog with a very old, very shitty trick."

Raisa shrugs. "This is Edinburgh, mate. You think you're going to be plastered over the front pages for one foul-mouthed faux pas? We should be so lucky to get that kind of publicity."

"I thought you said the press were invited."

"Just for the previews, my darling. Trust me, no one will give a bouncy turd about the unfortunate return of Cat, dead these long years. Just..." She reaches out and straightens his lapel, a gentle echo of something else that has been dead these long years, and he can see that she's also remembering when their relationship was more than it is now. "Just focus on the new material," she says. "Stick to your guns, old son, and you'll be fine."

Charlie is unable to respond right away, his throat suddenly constricted by emotion. The older he gets, the more prone he's become to such sneak attacks, it seems. He never used to care much about the ups and downs of his career, but now there's less time than there used to be. Now it really fucking matters. He blows out, turns it into a laugh.

"Man, I'm such an arsehole."

"You are," Raisa says with a smile. "But you're a bloody funny one."

He's saved from having to answer that by the vibration of his phone. He frowns at the unknown number, then swipes up. "Hello?"

"Yeah, Charlie, it's me."

If the number was unfamiliar, the voice isn't, although it's been some years since he last heard it. He listens to what his sister has to say, which is characteristically brief and blunt. When the call is over, he stares at the phone, finding it impossible to believe how easily the past can intrude into the present after all the effort he's put into separating the two. But then he's already had a lesson in that tonight, hasn't he?

"You all right, bab?" Raisa asks.

"Yeah, yeah, fine," he answers. "My mum's dead."

---

"Not to cast aspersions on such a solemn occasion," Raisa peers out through the rain-mazed windscreen, "but your hometown is unbelievably grim." The wipers sweep and swipe but fail to improve the view. A dented street sign slides by. *Burnshaw Road*. Charlie has no memory of that name, but he knew tons of dingy, redbrick streets like it. Not everything is the same though. There used to be grocers and hardware shops, barbers, bookies and off licences. Proper businesses. Now there are just low budget convenience stores, their windows filled with junk, desperate to try and sell something. Anything. *Fuck, it was never* this *bad*, Charlie thinks, with a swallow of guilt. As if, had he stayed, he would have done anything to prevent Morsley's decline.

Raisa is probably expecting a quip off him. Something cutting, the darker the better, but he's got nothing. He slumps in his seat. "You remember Covid?" he says quietly. "And Brexit? On top of the austerity years that we all suffered through, regardless of how we voted, but were absolutely self-inflicted in these parts. Well, Morsley was a shite hole before any of that."

He wasn't long out of his teens when he got out, a gleeful Shawshank escapee. After learning his trade on the local pub circuit, he'd started sending out C90 tapes of his routines. One, incredibly, had come back; and with it, like an actual chocolate factory golden ticket, an invitation to audition for a comedy club in London. He'd never looked back after that, nor ever wanted to. He might not even have returned for the funeral if Raisa hadn't stepped in to make the arrangements. He wonders if she's regretting that kindness now.

"Everyone comes from somewhere," she mutters, easing the car up to a red light at a complicated junction he's sure they've passed through already. "What does the satnav say? How close are we to the hotel?"

He peers at the dashboard screen. The dot that is them, the flag that is their frustratingly elusive destination. It would have been easier to get the computer just to do its thing, but Raisa's got a bee in her bonnet about *being told what to do* and won't have the voice on. He's useless with technology though, and with everything on his mind right now he's in no mood to struggle with it. But, after all she's done for him, how churlish would it be to refuse?

"Five minutes, maybe?" he guesses. "Second exit through the junction and then third on the left, I think."

"You think?" As the lights change, Raisa guns the engine, propelling them forward.

"Well, it originally wanted to send us down the one-way, didn't it? And then there was the roadworks. So, yeah…I think." He hates how petulant he sounds but can't help it. His emotions are all over the shop. He's spent most of the journey trying to work out how he feels about all this. It's not that he's glad his mum's dead, really. Given how much he came to hate her for all the stuff she put in his head, he's surprised to find that he doesn't have any feelings about her passing at all. He severed contact so long ago that it's like she's been dead for years.

On the other hand, being back in Morsley is giving the old emotions a proper stirring up.

"Jesus, Charlie," Raisa mutters. "Don't ever let anyone tell you… *fuck!*" When she stamps on the brake, they grunt in unison as their seatbelts punch the wind from them. The car stalls with a shudder.

"Did you fucking see that?" Raisa wheezes. She's staring furiously towards the pavement, where a lass in a sodden parka is standing at the kerb, staring sullenly back at her. "Little fucker's not even going to cross, is she?" Raisa looks like she's about to get out and give the kid both barrels but someone behind honks their horn, so instead she jerks the car mobile again. "Did you see her though? Stepped right out and she was looking right at me when she did it." As they pull away her eyes flick to the rear-view mirror, "Oh, and *now* she crosses."

Charlie chews his lip, suddenly gripped with the sensation that he's fraying, coming apart. "I saw her," he says.

"Oh, you did?" Raisa pumps the gas, eyes like coals on the verge of ignition. "Is it normal round here to just walk out into the fucking traffic?"

He could tell her that, yes, that is a thing they actually do here. A local tradition. When they want to cross the street – *look left, look right, look left again* – they intentionally step out in front of cars and then jump back onto the pavement. It's terrifying. Why does she think he doesn't bloody drive? He *could* tell her that, but what would be the point? It'd raise too many other questions, and they're only here until the funeral's over. They'll be back in London by dinner time tomorrow.

"It's this one," he says instead.

"What?"

"The turning." She's still riding the accelerator. "*This one*, Raisa!"

"Fuck." She brakes and wrenches the wheel to the left, and the sophisticated Merc somehow smooths all of that out into an easy arc, and now they're barrelling along a street called *Herries Terrace*. Opposing rows of residential two-up-two-downs. Scabby brickwork. Tiny, grubby gardens. A soiled St George's flag plastered to an upstairs window. "You sure this is right?"

He's watching their dot jerk along the sat-nav screen. "According to this…"

The row of houses on the right abruptly gives way to a brutal 1970s concrete façade with several floors of fly-spackled windows that can only, miracle of miracles, be the back of the hotel. Below is a small car park, a rusty barrier pole pointing to the glowering sky.

Entering the car park, Raisa eases her shiny black motor into a space beside a silver Polo with a flat tire and a roof caked in pigeon shit.

"Here we are then," she says lightly as she gets out and opens the back to grab her overnight bag, but

Charlie doesn't miss the sneer of disgust that briefly creases her features.

"Yeah." He slides out and retrieves his own suit bag. The car door closes with a gentle but definite click. "Welcome to Morsley."

———

"The dhal is all right, actually." Raisa takes a second helping before nudging the tarnished silver-plated dish Charlie's way. She's picked at the gluey madras, barely touched the luminous rice, and not even so much as acknowledged the existence of the greasy, blackened naan.

Charlie can't blame her. It is a truly terrible restaurant. Given the abuse the Asian communities always got around here, he can only assume it remains in business out of pure spite. He passes the dhal back. At the very least she's earned the lion's share of what's edible.

"Yeah, sorry." Even as he says it, he recognises that he's taking responsibility for something he can do nothing about and hears his therapist's gentle admonishment in his head. *Not your community, Charlie. Not anymore. That's all in the past.* They're only here because it's sheeting down out there and this place was closest to the hotel. Besides, they could have wandered for ages looking for something better, and only got wetter.

What he's actually sorry for is that she feels obliged to be here at all. "Look," he says. "I really appreciate this."

Raisa looks up from scooping curried lentils onto a papadum. "What do you mean, bab?"

"I mean driving me here, coming with me tomorrow..."

"Well, you don't drive, and in our fifteen-year professional relationship I've heard every one of the zillion reasons you don't like trains. So it was the easiest way." She takes a bite, swallows. "And you looked like you could do with a bit of support," she says more gently. "What else are friends for?" For a second she looks uncharacteristically bashful, then she catches herself. "I still care about your welfare, Charlie. Someone has to."

"Thanks." It's inadequate, but he doesn't know what else to say. He puts a piece of chicken in his mouth and thinks of England. It's aggressively spicy and stubbornly resistant to chewing, and it takes half of his remaining lager to swill it down.

"Do you want to talk about her?" Raisa says. "I mean I always knew you didn't get on and, much as I love a bit of gossip, God knows I don't want to pry for the sake of it. But...well, if ever there's a time..."

He glances up, surprised, though he oughtn't to be. In the brief time they were a sort-of couple, he'd been immediately accepted into Raisa's generous, loving family, and from the start it became awkwardly obvious how determined he was to avoid the subject of his own. Even her alarmingly forthright *nani* gave up asking eventually.

"Well, yeah," he says. "We were...estranged." *Estranged.* Fuck's sake. What a weird, inadequate word for the gulf between himself and the stubborn little nugget that Brenda Mason had been. The matriarch, not only of Charlie's own family, but of the entire Chilwell Estate he grew up on. If you wanted a benefits loophole you went to Bren for the inside track. If some tart was trying it on with your bloke, you went to Bren and she'd set her right in no uncertain terms. If you didn't like the look of your new neighbours, you went to Bren and she'd mobilise a mob to hound them out. Double quick if they had the wrong accent or skin colour.

If you wanted a mind filled with poison and prejudice, all you had to do was grow up her kid.

Of course, it wasn't just random bile. Everything came with a justification. *We got precious little*, she used to say to him and Lesley, *and what we got we had to fight for. We look after our own here cos no other bastard will*. Such sentiments were augmented and amplified into belligerent truths by the friends and neighbours up and down the estate's grey streets.

She'd been like a guru of hatred. And she'd been worshipped for it.

It took years living out in the real world for Charlie to recognise that the notoriety of his early career as a national gobshite, though lucrative, was really not something to be proud of, and to begin to understand how damaging his mother's influence had been. *Where did the Cat come from?* his therapist had repeatedly asked, without ever really getting an answer, because Charlie himself didn't know.

Regardless, Charlie had eventually managed to remediate himself enough to jettison the thing that had made him famous and go back to the beginning. Starting from scratch had been hard but, when it didn't work out, he'd tried again. And again. What else is he supposed to do?

"She was that bad?" Raisa says in answer to his silence.

Charlie drains his pint. It goes down like acid, but he tries to catch the eye of the waiter for another anyway. The lad is maybe still of school age. He has a bum-fluff moustache and white shirt a size too large with a long turmeric stain like a skidmark down the front, and he's going around the empty tables lighting candles in red jars. At each one he takes a second to rattle the matchbox – *shake, shake, shake* – before extracting the match.

"Charlie?"

Charlie hears the scritch, waits for the flare. *It's dangerous to play with matches.*

Raisa cranes around to see what he's looking at. "What's he doing?"

"What?"

"That boy. What's he doing?"

Charlie blinks. "It's just a local…superstition."

"Like the road crossing thing?"

"Yeah," he says. "Like that. They're fond of their superstitions round here."

He gathers himself. It's time to say the big thing that he's been working up to.

"Look, you don't have to come tomorrow. To the funeral, I mean. I'll be fine. It's just for a few hours."

"It's really no trouble." Raisa's brow creases in concern. "I came all this way after all."

"I just don't want you to feel like an outsider," he says lamely. "The family are pretty…close knit."

Raisa concentrates on wiping her fingers on her napkin for a moment. Then she says, "Is that a euphemism for 'racist' by any chance?"

"Just a little," he says, grateful as ever for her ability to read the script. And for not bringing up Edinburgh again.

"I can handle it," she says. And, when he raises his hands in demurral, "I said I can handle it, Charlie. For a few hours." Tossing back her wine, she grimaces. "But dinner is on you."

They settle up and go outside to find that the rain has stopped. There's a weary atmosphere about the place that feels like a lull in battle. Overflowing gutters drip and splash. Thirsty drains gulp and rush. Under the fizzling streetlights, the parked cars look submerged. Behind the cars an advertising hoarding displays an image of a manically smiling family above the cheerfully incomprehensible acronym, YIDO. Strips have been torn from the weathered poster. They look like claw marks and beneath the hoarding, Charlie thinks he sees something lithe slinking, but though he stares into the shadows a few seconds longer, he doesn't see it again.

Further along, they have to cross the street to return to the hotel. Without thinking, he steps onto the road, rocks back onto the pavement and then crosses for real. Raisa doesn't mention it, but he knows she saw.

---

Hotels like to advertise themselves as homes away from home. In Charlie's experience from his touring years, that's never true. Regardless of the trappings – from the thread count of the linens, to the fanciness of the toiletries, to the menu of services available in the health suite – every hotel room is ultimately merely a place for you stew in your own thoughts until it's time for breakfast. At least this hotel belongs to a chain. If he doesn't think too hard, he could be anywhere in the country. Anywhere but here.

He flicks through the TV channels – news, sports, sitcoms – before he comes across a BBC4 retrospective of the career of Mickey Greene. He knew Mick when they were both starting out on the alternative circuit, but they'd drifted apart. Charlie's surprised to discover that Mick is now mostly famous for writing children's books and occasionally being an independent voice of sanity tossed in amongst the politicians on *Question Time*. The bit about his behind-the-scenes involvement with Comic Relief is the point at which Charlie's had enough. He jabs at the remote, eventually settling on an old movie: *The Omega Man*, which features Charlton Heston doing his usual alpha male bit as he tries to help a band of survivors find a cure for a plague that turns people into mutants. He hasn't seen the movie since the teenage years he spent working his way methodically through the contents of the video rental shop at the corner of Montford Road. He remembers being scared of these pallid ghouls, but now it's not so much their hokey makeup that unnerves him as their slavish eagerness to follow their leader's agenda. As the movie drags on, he thinks about the futility of the movie trope of the hero. How ridiculous is the expectation that one man can save everyone just by being brave or hard enough, even Charlton Heston. By the end of the movie, Chuck will die to give the survivors an unlikely opportunity to survive for a while longer, but ultimately the audience knows they're doomed. Chuck should just have got out of there while he had the chance. Saved himself the grief.

Under the burble of tyre squeal and gunfire, there's a tentative knock at the door of Charlie's room. His hand hovers over the remote. The volume's about as low as it can go, so it can't be someone complaining about the noise. Besides, he knows this knock. It's the one that in the past has led to brief comfort and long regrets. And hasn't he got more than enough of those already?

He continues watching the black-cloaked mutants die. The knock isn't repeated.

The rain returns, bolstered now by a squally wind. It shakes the window in its aluminium frame and the streetlamps outside cast strange, jerky shadow patterns across the ceiling. As Charlie drowses, tomorrow finally seeps into the corners of his thoughts. He's going to have to face them, Lesley and all the rest. The boy who fucked off and got famous and lived it large by turning his upbringing into comedy capital while Morsley circled the drain. He reminds himself sternly that he should never regret severing those ties. It was what he'd needed to do to become a decent person. And, that one panicky lapse up in Edinburgh aside, he really, honestly believes that he is.

Charlie wonders who they are expecting to turn up tomorrow. He's no celebrity, not anymore. He's no Mickey fucking Green with a career that morphs effortlessly from one state to the next. They won't care if he tells them that he's rebuilding. Again, sure *again*. But he still has a talent for talking, and his new material is good. It's relevant for once. It's *honest* and for the first time since he can remember, he's fucking proud of it. In fact, now he's thinking about it with something like actual clarity, he realises he should be pushing it even further. He shouldn't just be erasing the Cat from his past in favour of revisiting those times through contemporary eyes. He should be using it as the *focus*. Spearing the moggy's festering ghost once and for all. It's so obvious, and it would work. There could even be a book in it for him. Not a kids' one, either. A proper one. He wishes he'd let Raisa in after all. Not for sex or comfort, but for this. She'd be thrilled to know that all of her efforts have been actually worth it.

Beyond the gusting rain and the *shruush* of late night cabs on the wet streets, and the intermittent distant explosions that tell him that kids still fool around with fireworks round here, Charlie thinks he hears an echo of an echo. A long, challenging *rrrrrowwwllll* that he knows is wholly imaginary, but nevertheless grips his heart and twists it.

---

*Wogan*, Series 9, Episode 19 (TX 17/3/1989)

*TW: Tell us about growing up. Did you have a happy childhood?*
*CM: I don't want to talk about that.*

# Death's Not As Funny
# As It Used To Be

In the car outside the crematorium, it occurs to Charlie how much worse funerals are on sunny days, their awfulness somehow magnified. With the puddles left by the rain rapidly shrinking, the mourners filing inside are sporting shades with their shabby black, their handkerchiefs dabbing at brows more than at eyes. There are few discernible hints of grief. Instead, there are handshakes, smiles, the occasional friendly laugh. Charlie recognises no one, though he must surely have known some of the older folks at least when he lived here. His stomach clenches like a rusty spring. What if he fails to recognise his own family? Last he saw any of them was that time Lesley brought the boys up to London and they had a pub lunch near the Borough Market. It hadn't exactly been a fun afternoon, quickly devolving into a shouting match between the adults that eventually got them asked to leave. What had the kids been then? Seven and nine? That would make them in their twenties now.

Man, this was such a mistake. Lesley's phone call had been an obligation to propriety, no more. There's no way they're actually expecting him to turn up.

Raisa's hand covers his own, stilling his frantically drumming fingers. "You okay?"

"Just another minute or two."

"It's due to start. Aren't there people you want to say hello to first?"

He shakes his head. "We'll just slip in at the back, eh?"

Her warm hand squeezes his. "Whatever you want, bab."

Only once the last of the crowd has trickled into the pebble-dashed building do Charlie and Raisa follow. Inside, the pews are all full, but they find a place near the door to stand. Again, Charlie is struck by the mood. In the rare moments he ever cared to imagine this day, he pictured the room all but empty, with only his mother's closest adherents there to shed what few tears she might be due. This place is packed and the mood is, if anything…expectant. There's a *buzz*. He's glad to be close to the exit, and now just wishes it would start so it can be over as soon as possible and let him be on his way.

Someone's meaty fingers yank Charlie's sleeve. "Here he is." The owner of the fingers and the grating, local accent is a young man with a florid complexion and blond hair that is floppy on top but shaved so hard in at the back and sides that the skin is an angry red above the collar of his shirt. "Mum, I've found him."

It's one of Lesley's boys, of course, but which? Charlie can barely picture those two scrappy tykes in that London pub, pinching each other while their overpriced burgers grew cold.

"All right, uh…Gary?" His guess isn't corrected. "I'm sorry for your loss, mate."

The lad doesn't acknowledge the ironic dissonance of Charlie saying those words to him, not the other way around, just nods his thanks. Gary's gaze then travels to Raisa waiting respectfully nearby, before whipping back to Charlie. His pink brow furrows. "Mum," he shouts again, and this time everyone in the crematorium turns to stare. Recognition ripples around the sea of strangers. Some of them get to their feet, their faces lighting up in a way Charlie hasn't seen since he was touring theatres. He was expected after all.

From the assembly's midst, his little sister appears. Lesley is short, like their mother was, though not as stocky. Instead of the severe jacket and polo neck combo old Bren would have favoured, Lesley has on a simple black dress, her freckled shoulders bare, and she's wearing a daisy chain around her neck.

"Cutting it fine there, weren't you?" Lesley says, though with more humour than scorn. Her hand slipping into his own feels natural and human as she tugs him forward. "Come on, everyone's waiting."

He resists the pull. "Oh no, I'm fine back here."

"Your place is front and centre with your family. We want you with us."

"Honestly, I'm fine." Pulling free, he glances at Raisa who, after all the build-up to this moment, looks as confused as he is.

"It's okay." Raisa smiles uncertainly. "I'll be fine here."

Charlie really doesn't want to go, but the beaming expectation on all these faces is not to be denied, so he allows himself to be led through the crowd. It's just a funeral, he tells himself and, like it or not, they *are* his family. He feels hands gentling his arms, patting his back. He guesses it's meant to be consolatory, but it feels weirdly reverential, and he thinks he's beginning to understand. Age hadn't withered Bren Mason. She'd remained as popular as ever in these parts. This is a *celebration*, and as her progeny, he's part of it whether he likes it or not. He feels nauseated, but it's too late to back out without making a scene.

At the front, Charlie takes the place that has been reserved for him between his sister and another young man who can only be her other son, Eric. Eric has a bright yellow dandelion flower pinned to the lapel of his jacket, as does the young woman next along who beams unnervingly at Charlie. Beside her is a toddler, who he takes to be their daughter. She is wearing Peppa Pig dungarees and on top of her blond curls rests a daisy chain tiara. Her big eyes blink a little sleepily in the subdued lighting.

As soon as they're all settled, the celebrant comes forward. A balding, middle-aged bloke in a dark suit and a purple shirt with no tie, he reminds Charlie of a cabaret MC. He bears no sign of religious affiliation, and neither is there any mention of God when he begins to speak, but in all other respects the cadence and flow of his speech are in keeping with the standard traditions. Remember. Celebrate the life. Forgive the human mistakes. It's all perfectly normal after all, perfectly mundane.

Relaxing a little, Charlie finally acknowledges the coffin on the roller belt in front of them. It bears no bouquets, no floral arrangements spelling out BRENDA or MUM. Instead, dandelions and daisies have been randomly strewn across the gleaming wood. Charlie blinks, his breath hitching as the significance of the flowers comes to mind. Bren Mason's often quoted words, declaimed in her iconic Superkings bray. *The weeds shall flourish.*

The proceedings have paused and the celebrant is smiling benignly at him. *What* did he just say? Charlie mentally rewinds a few seconds.

"Eulogy?" he blurts. "I…no, that's a mistake. I'm not doing any eulogy."

"You're the eldest," Lesley whispers. "It's expected."

"You're the man," says Eric with horrendously misplaced confidence.

"But I've not prepared anything." Charlie's face is suddenly hot, his mouth arid. He loosens his collar, but it doesn't help.

The celebrant nods reassuringly. "Just say what's in your heart. That's what she'd want."

Charlie's pretty fucking sure the last thing Bren Mason would want to hear at her own send-off would be what's in her son's heart, but the expectation in the room is intense now. Blinding, withering.

He stands and goes over to the lectern. "Right," he says, his brain scrambling to throw together some words that will appease his audience. *This is the gig*, he tells himself. *Just improv it to hell.* It doesn't matter if it's all lies, just as long as it sounds sincere.

He manages to lay out an honest beginning. "My mum and I didn't get along so well. But I'd like to think…" And that's as far as he gets. It's too hot. The audience's faces are flushed, their demand overwhelming. "I'd…" he tries to clear his throat, "…like to think…" Sweat beads on his brow, a drop rolling into the corner of his eye. Blinking the salty sting away, he closes his eyes to think. Just a few words. Just put them together.

He tilts his head to the side and senses someone standing next to him. Someone who whispers into his ear a jumble of yowling syllables.

"I'd like to think," even without a mic, Charlie's voice booms, "that everyone here knows how much of a fucking legend Brenda Mason was."

The crowd goes wild.

———

Afterwards, Charlie finds himself fending off handshakes and claps on the back as if he's just given them all the best night out of their lives. Shit, there was even a cheer as the curtain closed on the coffin. But that's not nearly the worst of it, he thinks, as he shoves his way through the crowd, a bubble of anxious vomit burning in his throat. He needs to find Raisa, needs to tell her that, whatever she heard him say just then, he didn't mean any of it. Not a word. It was just another lapse brought on by the pressure of the situation. The Cat, at his side, filling his mouth with awful filth. Just like the old days.

He's never been able to explain, not even to Raisa, how much it feels like that's exactly what happens – that there's really someone standing there, just out of sight, squawking out the most offensive things which he is compelled to repeat. Years ago, he'd have shamefacedly laughed it off, but not anymore. If he's learned one thing from the hard labour of his rehabilitation, it's to own his shit.

So, right now, yeah, he's not only alarmed at how flimsy his rebuilt foundations have yet again proved, but also deeply ashamed. At least it's over with. They can get in the car now and hightail it the fuck out of here.

Almost at the door now, but he still can't see Raisa. Likely she made a quick exit and will be waiting for him outside. Maybe even early enough to have missed his little performance. Could he be that lucky?

Emerging, blinking into the sunshine, he scans the milling crowd. Every smiling face is a white one. "Raisa?" he calls, counting along the line of vehicles to where they parked. Her car's not there either. He tells himself it doesn't mean anything. The mourners for the next service are already gathering. Maybe she's considerately shifted her car to free up a space. "Raisa!"

"Something the matter, Uncle Charlie?" As Eric approaches, he hoists the little girl in his arms. She looks even more tired than before after all the excitement. In the sunlight, Charlie notices now that one side of his nephew's face is marked, an angry curdling of the skin from neck to cheekbone. The ear lobe is deformed too. He wonders briefly what might have happened but dismisses it as a distraction. He has more important priorities.

"I'm looking for Raisa," Charlie says. "My friend?"

"Didn't see her, sorry," Eric says, then he calls over to his brother. "Gaz, you seen Uncle Charlie's friend?"

"The paki?" Charlie's use of that word in Edinburgh had been like dropping a grenade into the room. Here, as it ever was, it's shockingly unremarkable. "Yeah, I think she left."

"You can't call her that," Charlie says it automatically but without conviction, considering what came out of his own mouth not fifteen minutes ago. The cocktail of shame and cowardice brings the hot sourness surging back up again. He swallows anxiously. He just wants to be away from here. "Do you know where she went?"

Gary just smirks and turns away muttering something that Charlie isn't supposed to catch, though it might have been, *fucked if I care, mate*, before announcing to the gathering, "Right everyone, back to The Oswald for a lunch and a lock-in. Just like Nan would of wanted, yeah?"

As the crowd starts to drift towards the cars, Charlie scans for Raisa again. She can't have left. She wouldn't. She said she could deal with a frosty reception, a few fruity comments… but she'd not been prepared to hear them coming out of Charlie's mouth, had she? Not so soon after Edinburgh. She'd trusted his word, his promises. How many second chances even are there in the world?

He shouldn't have come back here. He's fucked everything.

Starting to panic, Charlie finally remembers to check his phone and, sure enough, there's a missed message from Raisa. No voice, just a text. *Gone back to the hotel. See you later.*

He stares at the message, unable to interpret it. It lacks the familiar *Rxx* at the end, but neither is there outright accusation. It's impossible to tell if she's angry or if it's just that something urgent came up with work. The *see you later* is promising, at least. He clings to it, picturing her in their hotel's tiny lounge, drinking coffee and setting up bookings. Edinburgh didn't go so badly after that first show. There'd even been an interview and snippet of his act on BBC Radio in a segment about comedy's so-called Woke Wave. The gross irony, apparently, passing the irritatingly youthful presenters by. On the journey down, Raisa had told him she was going to try and get him on a few bills around London to build momentum. There'd been enquiries, she said, though he'd suspected that was a white lie to bolster confidence, but maybe, right? Maybe?

As positive takes go it is gossamer thin. He needs to see her, to apologise and explain that it's this place. These people. It's not *him*. She knows how hard he's worked to make that so. It sounds pathetic, even in his own thoughts, but that's where they are. A basket case of a reformed right-wing stand-up, and a manager with too big a heart for her own good.

Eric's at his elbow again. "Ready to go?" he says. "The pub isn't far."

Charlie is disarmed by the lad's quiet amiability, but he's made up his mind. This lot have had more than their money's worth from him.

"Sorry," he says. "I need to hook up with Raisa and get back to London. Work, you know?" Eric's wife joins them, her smile faltering as she overhears his obvious excuses. Charlie rushes on. "It's been nice meeting you both. And..." he tousles the toddler's hair, "this little treasure too, of course."

"But you haven't any transport," Eric's wife says.

Charlie waves his phone. "I'll get an Uber. It's fine."

"You won't get one of them in Morsley, London lad," the young woman scoffs. "Usually, your best bet'd be Sterling Cabs, but there's a match on today so you'll have a proper wait. Couple of hours, more than likely." Then she brightens. "Let us give you a lift."

"Oh no, really." Charlie tries to keep it nonchalant. "I wouldn't want to put you out."

"It's no trouble." She fishes car keys out of her bag and holds them out for her husband to take. "What hotel you in?"

"Uh." The pair seem genuinely well-intentioned so, reluctantly, he says, "the Travelodge, near the train station?"

"Well, that's perfect!" she says. "It's hardly even out of our way, right E?"

Eric, who is playing with the child, smiles. "Course," he says. "No problem. We're parked over here."

Charlie follows them to a dusty red Nissan sporting a roof box festooned with stickers advertising English resorts. Names of yesteryear, briefly in fashion for the pandemic staycation renaissance, but just as quickly out of favour again. He almost smiles at the thought of a young family like this taking vacations in Margate and Whitstable before remembering that people round here often aren't the biggest fans of holidaying in Europe. He watches Eric place his daughter – Summer, he learns – into the car seat in the back, the child's big, trusting eyes widening as her dad chats quietly away to her. Kids are like that, aren't they? They soak everything up. That thought hollows Charlie, but it's none of his business, and saying something will only lead to grief.

Charlie gets in beside Summer while the other two adults climb into the front. In sync, they reach for their seatbelts but, instead of securing them, allow the tongues to slip out of the slots, the belts retracting behind their seats again. It's another Morsley thing. Like the kerb, like the matches. Tempting fate, sticking your hand up to get its attention because sure as hell you've got no one else's. He shakes his head and engages his own belt properly. As the car starts to move, he sees the harness clasp of Summer's chair hanging loose too and leans over to fix it. He can do that at least.

As they drive, Eric's wife, whose name is Keli and who is a nurse, twists herself around to talk at him in a rattling hail of natter, pausing only for the seconds it takes to suck her cigarette into life. She has the window open, but she waves her hands around so much that most of the smoke wafts through to the back seat. Her daughter's eyes are watering, but the smoke is far from the biggest reason that Charlie now regrets accepting this lift.

"Busting an immigrant paedo ring in the corrupt, bastard BBC!" Keli grins at him. "Killed me, man. That's classic Bren, that is. Isn't it, E? Classic Bren."

Eric, concentrating on driving, nods. "Classic Nanna, yeah."

Charlie's mouth is dust dry. During the travesty masquerading as a eulogy, he'd related a story about Bren's campaign against the presenters of a regional radio show dedicated to Asian music. Though based on a kernel of actual memory, he'd inflated it into a horrible, aggrandizing fiction. The last thing he wants to do is discuss any of his performance's finer points, but Keli is fired up.

"I mean," she goes on, tapping her ash on the window rim, "it's like that routine you did on Parkinson in, whassit, E, ninety-one? Something like that?"

"Something like, yeah," Eric replies. He's a quiet lad, a still pool counterbalancing his wife's froth.

There should have been a sign for the station by now. Charlie's been looking out for it, but is distracted for the moment by Keli's reference to an ill-fated chat show appearance that must have taken place before she was born.

"You've seen my old routines?" he says, despite himself.

"Ha! Yeah, man. Have we ever? Gary transferred them to the computer from Bren's old VHSs. She was well proud of you. *Tells like it is, that boy,* she always said."

Charlie doesn't know how to deal with this information. He's always relied on the fact that many of his worst offences took place before the dawn of the present internet and cell phone age where nothing now is ever forgotten or forgiven. He hopes to God none of his club shows survived. The TV ones were *Play School* material by comparison.

He remembers that Parkinson appearance, though. He'd been laying hard into the green room hospitality for the best part of an hour before the host came by to introduce himself. Parkie had been pleasant enough and Charlie remembers thinking they were getting on quite well, but his parting shot as he went out to start the show, delivered in those famous, fatherly Yorkshire tones, had been just patronising enough to light the touchpaper. *Try not to be too controversial, son.* So, that had been the night Cat had come up with...

"Nonce Corner," Keli laughs. "Utter genius, man. Totally called it on Savile that night. Though, of course, them Yewtreers were just sacrificial lambs to protect the establishment, weren't they? They're the proper fucking scum." Unbidden, Summer laughs and Keli grins at her. "That's right in't it, babes. The leftie establishment are all fucking scum. Riddled with little brown, paedo slugs, in't they? Ruining our England."

Summer smiles blissfully and, once more, Charlie prays she's too young to understand what she's hearing. He knows he ought to say something, but before he can do so he hears the *tick-tick* of the indicator, and feels the car ease over to the side of the road. The trickle of relief Charlie feels at the journey coming to an end dries up when he glances out and sees that they're not at his hotel. Instead, they're parked next to an aggressively traditional looking pub. It has mullioned windows and a panelled frontage painted pillar box red. The fancy writing above the door reads: *The Oswald*.

"Sorry, Uncle Charlie," Eric says. "We've got the sandwiches in the boot and in this heat…well, best to drop them off before they turn, eh?"

"Yeah, that's fine," Charlie says, although it is anything but fine, plausible though the excuse is. "I'll wait here with Summer."

"Will you hell," says Keli, getting out and coming round to extract the little girl from her chair. "This one's coming in too, and there's loads of bags to carry."

"Just five minutes, Charlie, eh?" Eric at least is capable of embarrassment, the skin around his scars flushing a little pinker. "Mum'll want to say goodbye."

Charlie feels angry at being manipulated, but what can he do? He doesn't know where he is. Raisa would look it up, but Charlie doesn't know how to do that. He stays away from search engines on principle.

And Eric's right. Under the circumstances, he ought to speak to Lesley. Have it out with her about what happened at the service…and maybe, finally, clear the air and let them all move on. Who knows when they'll get another chance? He can do that at least. He'll call Raisa first, tell her what's happening and that he'll get back to the hotel as soon as he can. It won't be the five minutes Eric is optimistically promising, but half an hour should do it, tops. He can ask the pub staff for directions.

"All right." He unbuckles his seat belt, gets out of the car and is immediately handed several supermarket carrier bags bulging with sandwiches and multipacks of crisps.

Inside the pub, he finds a long oak bar with traditional brass pumps, faded St George's bunting left over from the last football tournament, lincrusta walls the colour of oxblood Doc Martens, and an absolute throng of people. Everyone who was at the crematorium must have come on for the social, and brought a couple of friends each into the bargain. His heart flips until he realises that the fervour from earlier has dissipated. It's now more like a normal family gathering than some sort of evangelistic revivalist meeting. He wonders if, in his panic, his imagination had exaggerated the scenario earlier. According to his therapist, his imagination has been responsible for a lot of things.

While the packets of sandwiches and crisps are lined up along the bar, someone presses a glass of scotch into Charlie's hand. He manages to savour one well-earned sip before the crowd spots him. Surrounded, he freezes at first before the automatic pilot routine perfected during his brief popularity on the showbiz party circuit kicks in. But it turns out it's not necessary. The mourners are friendly, respectful even. Condolences are heartfelt and couched with sensitivity to his and his mum's relationship. And far from fawning, they appear genuinely interested in how his career is going. In no time at all, he finds himself slipping from smile-and-nod to real conversation. To reconnecting. There are cousins, with stories of their own. Schools and families. Matches, hatches and dispatches. Every time he reaches for his glass, it has been refilled. He's getting quite drunk and that's no bad thing, because it's helping him get past his prejudices. To realising that the likes of Gary and Keli are the outliers, the Bren Mason superfans. The rest of them are just normal people, without even one Heart Of Britain badge among them. He starts to enjoy himself.

⁓

Charlie is coming out of the bogs when he remembers he hasn't called Raisa yet and, squinting at his phone, is horrified to see that he's been here for two hours. Raisa has neither called nor texted again, and that is unmistakably a sign that she's pissed off. There's no way they'll get back to London before rush hour now.

Charlie heads for the pub's main door but it won't open. "Shit a brick," he mumbles, his lips cumbersome from the whisky.

"You all right there?" It's Gary, his tie discarded and shirt sleeves rolled up for his stint as barman.

"The door?" Charlie says. "It's locked."

"No kidding." Gary laughs. "Well, that's the thing about lock-ins, in't it?"

"I suppose, yeah." Charlie hopes Gary will follow the wisecrack up by flourishing the keys from his pocket. He doesn't.

Instead, Gary nods at a narrow staircase that Charlie hadn't noticed before. "Mum wants to see you."

"What? Up...there?" Charlie's embarrassed by the reticence obvious in his voice. Wasn't making his peace with Lesley the whole point of coming here?

"Yeah." Gary's expression is nakedly contemptuous. "Give you both a bit of privacy, eh?"

"Right," Charlie says. "Only, I have to make this phone call first."

"No rush, mate." Gary laughs again. This time there's no humour in it. "Well, within reason. You know what Mum's like."

Charlie makes himself laugh back, sealing the deal. His mouth feels gluey. He needs to drink some water, but Gary's retreat back into the lounge offers him the best opportunity he'll have to call Raisa before something else happens. He taps up his contacts, goes to Favourites, puts the phone to his ear and listens. Five, six, seven rings. It goes to answerphone. He hangs up because Raisa always has her phone on her, always answers right away. He dials again. And again. After the fifth attempt, he accepts that she's ghosting him intentionally, and leaves a stumbling message full of apologies, promising to be back at the hotel as soon as he can, although even as he hangs up he's already contemplating with dread the possibility of having to take the train. If she's *really* angry, she might be halfway home already. He wouldn't blame her.

A wave of laughter breaks against the other side of the door that leads to the bar. It sounds like gulls, mocking. Charlie glances at the stairs, even now wondering if there's any way of avoiding this. Maybe he can persuade the more amenable of his nephews, Eric, to get hold of the keys and just let him be on his way... But, no, he has to do this. His...what? Penance? Is that what it is? A reckoning? If he owes his sister anything, it's that.

Charlie feels like an intruder as he climbs, flinching at every creak on the stairs. At the top, all the doors but one are shut. He crosses the landing and peers into the room beyond. With the curtains drawn, it is dark but for the illumination of a solitary lamp. It strikes him as oddly subterranean, like a grotto or something. Lesley is there, perched on the edge of a sofa and nursing a glass of red, the bottle by her feet. The lamp casts her in an unforgiving chiaroscuro that emphasises her thinness, how whittled she is. Beyond her, Charlie can just about make out a fireplace with a tiled surround and a framed mirror above the mantel, the dull rectangle of a TV and the hulk of an armchair. The ceiling and corners are swagged in shadow.

"You took your time," Lesley says, echoing her greeting at the crematorium, although there's a different inflection to it this time. The humour swapped for the bitterness he'd been expecting from the start.

"There was a lot of catching up to do," Charlie says, always the comedian. The corners of his sister's mouth tighten and he can't help doubling down. "Saved the best until last, obviously."

Lesley scoffs, drains her glass and refills it. Her hands are trembling. A sign of grief at last, perhaps.

"Look," Charlie blurts, reaching for platitudes even now in his attempt to forestall the confrontation, "you'll be okay. Brenda was a big character and it feels like she's left a massive hole but I promise you'll find a way of filling it."

Lesley's brow crinkles and at first he thinks she's going to cry before her expression instead furls in scorn. "Is that supposed to be a pep talk?" She takes another swig of wine. Her lips are dark with it. "We'll be fine if we all show a bit of community spirit? Fuck you, Charlie, seriously. Mum *was* the community. All those schemes she had on the go, all those balls in motion. All those people looking to her, depending on her. Then the cancer – oh, by the way, she died of cancers of the lung and oesophagus, thanks for caring enough to ask that simple, basic question – ripped even that from us. And guess who everyone expects to magically pick it all up and carry on?" She tosses her drink back, momentarily squeezing her eyes shut as if she's swallowing ground glass instead of merlot. "Fill the hole she left? It's *all* hole, mate. Course, it doesn't matter to you, does it? You can swan off back to your cushy London flat and forget all about it. *You* got out."

"It's not that cushy a flat," Charlie mumbles defensively, thinking about the draughty windows and mouldy bathroom ceiling he's never quite had the cash to fix. Immediately, though, he recognises how petty that thought is. For better or worse, he's not had to depend on Bren Mason to solve his problems. Which is the point, isn't it? His family, the community. When did he last even think about them? And why does he find, now, that some part of him cares?

He thinks about the gathering downstairs, about Eric and little Summer, who'll never get as lucky as Charlie did. Who'll have to make the best of what little life here offers them. Because, as a rule, people don't leave Morsley.

"Look," he says. "Maybe…I don't know…I could get Raisa to organise a benefit. Raise some funds for, maybe, a youth centre or something?"

Lesley rolls her eyes. "A fucking youth centre? You really are a comedian, aren't you? Mum was on the board of the South Morsley TeenZone community initiative for fifteen years, and I took over from her last year. Trust me, lack of youth centres are the least of our problems."

That stings because he was being earnest, but… yeah, he gets it. You'd think after all the benefits he's done, all the years listening to his leftie friends bang on about clueless entitlement, he'd recognise it when he saw it in the flesh. Fuck it, you could just make his "charity funded youth centre" the dictionary definition and be done with it. In the darkness he can feel his cheeks burning. She's right to be offended. Right to call him out as the outsider he is. He hasn't a clue.

And with that realisation, comes another. All these years he thought it was hate that was screwing him up, rage at how his upbringing had hobbled him. Now he recognises it, sealed off all this time like black water in a poisoned well, as…guilt. And it's beginning to seep out.

"Well, all right," he says. "Sorry. You say I don't care and I'm offering to help. Seriously. What do you need?"

Her mouth is a stitched line.

"Me? Oh, not much. Self-respect. Self-sufficiency. A ghost of a chance of finding a fucking job at my age so I don't end up on the scrounge the rest of my life. Same as anyone else really."

He understands better now. Brenda might have been a master at manipulating the benefits system, but she'd been even better at finding work for those in need. A word in the right ear could magic up a supermarket shift, a shop job from her ever growing network of favours and debts, and even in Morsley with its crippling unemployment rate her kids had never wanted for work. Before now. Lesley's despair is raw. A glimpse of the pressure on her, the expectation. She's not their mum. She knows it, and she's terrified.

"What happened to the car plant?" Charlie asks.

"Didn't you hear? They moved it to Belgium."

He bites his tongue on a knee-jerk crack about the fruits of Brexit. A quip like that'd have gone down well in Hoxton where the good old metropolitan elite are still pissed off about that lunacy, but not here. Here, the working class voted with selfishness but also with a naïve kind of hope, and they were well and truly fucked over for it. Charlie remembers what it was like growing up here under Thatcher. He can only imagine what living here is like now.

"You do remember the car plant, then," Lesley says.

Charlie nods. It had been a big deal at the time. A massive investment and a major boost to the town. Just about every family in Chilwell had depended on it to pay the rent.

"And you remember how it came about?"

There's an edge to those words that Charlie can't quite see, a hidden barb. "What do you mean?" he says warily.

"You know what I mean." Her face is pinched. "That little slice of luck that came just when we needed it most. You *know* how it came about."

Suddenly Charlie's heart is rattling around his chest like a caged sparrow because he knows what she's going to say. Something he'd boxed up and labelled as fantasy a long time ago.

"The trials," Lesley says. "The Golden Path."

"No," Charlie says quietly, because quietly is all he can manage. "That…wasn't real."

It's the first time he has spoken these words out loud to another person other than his therapist, although he has been intoning them like a catechism for years. Convincing himself that his own success had been down to talent and hard graft and had nothing to do with the crazy lore that had been spoon fed to him with his morning Shreddies. Nothing to do with the unbelievably horrible thing he did at the culmination of his fucked-up childhood. A memory he'd squeezed into the tiniest, darkest hole along with all of the other terrors. And there had been many of those because the seventies and eighties he'd grown up in had been a time of fear. Global nuclear annihilation was only ever the blare of a siren away, and on TV a series of grim, grainy public information films terrorised you with the potentially lethal consequences of almost everything in your day-to-day environment. With all of that getting wrapped up in Morsley's strange little traditions and then funnelled through Brenda Mason's own unique brand of high-pressure zeal, it was little wonder Charlie had ended up like he had. His therapist had only helped unpack a little of it. Enough for Charlie to get the perspective he needed. To understand that, if he'd just been patient, the casting call would have come anyway. That his life would have turned out exactly the same. That what he did that sunny afternoon had ultimately been as pointless as it had been evil.

But now Lesley is suggesting…what? That his cruelty had also been responsible for saving the town?

"It *was* real," she says matter-of-factly. "You made it happen. You got your big break, and we got the car plant."

"That doesn't make sense," Charlie says, because he knows that even if he admits the possibility that the ritual *had* been a real thing, his ask had only been for himself. One hundred percent selfish.

And, *fuck*, the memories are unfolding now, like black paper flowers. The five stations: The Road, The Lightning Factory, The Lake, The Stranger, and lastly The Tombs.

He can barely find his voice. "It was only a cat."

Lesley's laughter is horribly reminiscent of the animal's shrieks as he'd shut the door. "Is that what you thought all these years? That you got all that success from sacrificing a cat?"

"I didn't think anything," he says through gritted teeth. "Because it *wasn't real.*" He's surprised by his own vehemence, but he needs to keep on believing it because the fact that he was able to build one career on the back of his own efforts means he can do it again. If instead he *bargained* for his first big break, it means his future is fucked.

Lesley leans forward. "You remember Edward Pettifer?"

Taken by surprise, Charlie falters. That's a name he hasn't heard in decades. It conjures a vague picture of a weedy pre-teen from the houses up the back of the estate where the black families had lived.

"Swotty little berk, wasn't he?" he says warily. "Friend of yours from junior school? Until Mum found out."

And, yeah, now he remembers the row that day. *What in God's name is* that *doing in this house, girl? Just because he's got an English name doesn't make him British.* Though it horrifies him now, his mother's racism hadn't bothered him at the time. Nor had he given the boy another thought when he'd stopped coming round.

"That's right," Lesley says levelly. "And then?"

Charlie shakes his head, unwilling to make the link she's offering. "I don't know. I thought he'd just moved school or something."

"Edward ran away when he was fourteen," she says, a spark of something in the corner of her eye. "At least that's what everyone assumed."

Again, Charlie knows what she's going to say. He wants to stop it, but he can't.

"Edward Pettifer disappeared on the twenty-first of June, nineteen eighty-six."

"The same day…"

"The same day as you ran The Golden Path and bargained for our future."

*No, no, no.* It had just been Mrs Cooper's stinking old ginger tom. Just a *bloody cat.* But he can't escape the logic in her version of events, and he has to ask.

"What did you do, Lesley?"

Her eyes flash with the anger that she's been kindling all this time. All these years, in fact.

"I did what you wouldn't have had the guts to do. How much of a future would you have got for a cat, Charlie? We needed much more than that."

Charlie rubs his eyes, trying to stop it connecting, coalescing. "It's not a real thing," he says again. "If you really did that…" And to look at her he has no doubt she's telling what she believes to be the truth. "It was a fucking senseless waste."

He makes himself stop. Breathe. The room's gloomy shadows are wavering now as if there's something wrong with the bulb, though nothing else – the sofa, the chair, the mantel, the TV – looks different. The rumble of conversation from downstairs has been enhanced by muffled music. The world is still the world he knows. The world he has chosen to live in.

"What…" He tries to work out what he wants to say. "What are you telling me here?"

Lesley has lost some of her fire. "I'm asking for your help."

He shakes his head. "I already offered—"

"Not for some poxy comedy benefit. *Real* help." She goes to refill her wine glass again, but there's only a dribble left. The bottle drops to the carpet with a guillotine thud. "You have to follow the Path again."

"No." It's a gut response. Visceral. "No way."

He can't stop the memory flowers continuing to bloom in slow motion in his mind. Not just the stations now, but the details of what happened there.

"You have to, Charlie. It worked before."

"Then get someone else to do it."

"Don't you think we've tried?" The light makes her eyes appear to shiver. "Eric didn't get past the second station." She bites her lip. "And Andrew never even made it across The Road. We need *you*."

Charlie pictures Eric's scarred face. And then remembers Andrew, the boys' father. When Lesley and the kids had arrived in London for that visit, Charlie'd just assumed that their relationship to be in one of its off-again stages. He hadn't even asked. Looking back now, there had been such a fractious edge to that day, hadn't there? Another squirt of guilt. What she's asking, though...is impossible.

"I'm really sorry," he says, reaching over to touch her arm. She jerks away. "Look, I can send you some money or something, but that's it. I'll ring you in a couple of days. Right now, I need to meet up with Raisa and get back to London."

"Oh yeah," Lesley snarls, suddenly explosive again, "you kept that little surprise quiet, didn't you? Can't believe you ever thought Mum would have wanted one of them at her own funeral."

"What Mum might want," Charlie snaps, angry now too, "isn't relevant anymore. Raisa is my manager, and my friend..."

Lesley's expression turns cat sly. "Go on then. Call her now."

"I don't need to. I'll see her at the hotel—"

"Call your friend," she says. "Now."

And there is a heft in those deliberate words that makes him reach for his phone. He notices there are still no messages before thumbing up his contacts again. His finger hovers over the call button, suddenly very nervous. It's the fervour that has crept into Lesley's eyes that makes him commit.

He recognises the jarring ringtone right away but refuses to believe he's hearing it actually in the room. Not even when Lesley holds Raisa's phone out in its shocking pink cover, his own number flashing on the screen for a few more rings before it stops.

"I'm afraid Raisa's not able to answer right now," Lesley says in a scornfully cod posh-Birmingham voice.

"What have you done?" Charlie says.

"What we fucking had to."

# The Golden Path

*Points of View* (TX 25/11/1992)

Dear Anne

I am writing to express my disgust at the inclusion of so-called "alternative comic" Charlie Mason on last Friday's otherwise stellar Children In Need programme. As if his childish, foul-mouthed antics weren't objectionable enough, his ridicule of this country's much-loved public information safety films crossed the line of acceptability. Belittlement of these important educational messages is the last thing our children need!

Yours sincerely, Eleanor Wooding (Mrs)

---

*You can sit on your hands and say ta for the scraps you're given*, Brenda Mason used to say, *or you can stand up and fight for what's yours instead of it being dished out for free to every immigrant who steps off the boat. You can expect a bloody nose or two, sure, but the alternative is waiting till your dying day for things to get better. You have to walk The Golden Path, son, if you want your due.*

The Path had been part of Morsley longer than anyone could remember. It traversed a stretch of wooded dene and boggy meadow that never seemed to get developed or built on, and the town had grown around it, made it its dark heart. That crooked delta of land, bounded by an A-road on one side, the railway on another and the River Horn on the third, was a quiet, wild place visited only by druggies, doggers and fly tippers, and never for longer than their business required.

There was no easy way to get there either. As if, unable to put the land to profitable use, the town planners had instead conspired to make everyone forget that it existed. Yet it had persisted in Morsley's collective consciousness. In threats and promises, playground boasts and bedtime stories. As echoes in the myriad tics and superstitions people acted out daily without thinking. Everyone had heard of someone who was said to have attempted the ritual. The way Charlie's mum had talked, the rewards of the Path favoured only the bravest. Her fervour on the matter had naturally led her offspring to believe that she must have taken it on herself once upon a time, though she never actually came out and said so. Years later, as Charlie slowly and painfully extracted himself from the mental barbed wire of his upbringing, he'd finally understood that on this, as on many other subjects, his mother had been full of shit.

The trials awaiting you at each of the stations of the Path were stupidly dangerous. To actually go through with them you had to be naive, desperate, and have something to offer. Something you believed *they* would want. But people still made the attempt. Charlie had been one of them and, according to Lesley now, the only one in recent memory to have succeeded.

The little entourage making its way down through the Chilwell Estate is subdued. Ironically funereal at last, Charlie thinks, although it feels less like walking with his family so much as being escorted to the scaffold. The two women led from the front, Lesley pensive, Keli practically skipping across the cracked paving slabs of the little shopping parade. With evening approaching, the streetlights are stuttering on. In front of the shuttered shops that line two sides of the square, a pair of massive gulls are fighting over a morsel of food. Under the lights, they look like bareknuckle fighters, scrapping away at one of the unlicensed bouts they used to hold down at the old engine works on Parnel Street. The cars came past there on the way over. The ugly works sheds have been pulled down and it's just waste ground now. A bunch of light skinned Middle Eastern lads kicking a ball around elicited a comment from Keli about that part of town *not really being Chilwell any more anyway*. The estate is a shrinking territory.

So much has changed here. Entire streets of these dismal roughcast semis have metal sheeting over their windows and doors. From the blistered, faded menu in the window, it seems the square's old fish and chip shop became a kebab place at some point in the years since he and Lesley were routinely sent over here to get the family's dinner. Likely it changed hands dozens of times before its inescapable demise at the hands of the Deliveroo revolution. Like all the other units in the parade, it is permanently shuttered now.

Leaving the square, they take an unlit path that runs out through the back of the estate, Charlie following the women, the two brothers tagging on behind like minders. Charlie can hear Eric chatting softly away to Summer, who rides on his shoulders. The kid is getting fractious now. It's been a long day for her and, though she's borne it like a trooper, she's clearly flagging. Charlie doesn't even remember her getting fed save for the coke and crisps someone plonked in front of her in the pub.

As they walk on, Charlie looks down at his feet, at his good dress shoes built for London pavements not this disintegrating tarmac, at the grassy banks on either side thick with daisies and dandelions, the white and gold vivid in the gloaming. This is all wrong. He can't believe he's here, can't believe his sister capable of following through on her threats. Lesley isn't Brenda, he tells himself. All of this is just, what, a smokescreen? Lies born from desperation? That story she told him about Edward Pettifer was just some crap she made up to try and convince him she's serious. And they don't have Raisa. They've just stolen her phone to get him to go through with this madness. And he's not going to. No way.

Then he catches Lesley's eye and his resolve flies apart like dandelion seeds. He sees a darkness in her that wasn't there before.

*Andrew never even made it across The Road.*

He'd forgotten what it was like to live here. How it twists your thinking. And now he's wondering: if they *have* kidnapped Raisa, what's their plan? Images of her in the Tombs, scared in the dark with her air already running low, crowd at the corners of his imagination but...no, that doesn't make sense. She can't be the offer because the supplicant is supposed to bring that with them round the stations... Aren't they?

Charlie quickens his pace down the path, only to draw up short again when he sees that they are approaching the underpass that marks the boundary of the estate. The crumbling concrete, spray-painted the colours of decay, rebar protruding like rusting bones, looks like it might collapse at any moment, but his companions don't even hesitate before entering. The darkness is warm and acrid. Their footsteps resound off the walls. *Are you sure about this?* the echoes say. *You can still turn back.* Charlie wants more than anything to turn back, to go home and forget about all of this. But if there's even a chance that Raisa is in danger, how can he?

When they emerge, the oncoming evening seems darker, as if they were in the short tunnel an hour instead of a mere half a minute, but it must just be the spindly birches that line the path here crowding out the sky. Below the trees, the flowers are so profuse that they almost overgrow the path entirely. Golden heads brush the legs of Charlie's suit trousers and nod like gossips in his wake.

The path peters out at the foot of a steep bank. Charlie can't see the top, but he can hear the rumble and rush of the traffic. They've already reached the first station.

# The Road

"Wait up," he says, but they're already climbing. "This isn't going to work."

"It fucking has to, mate." Gary's right behind him. "Simple as."

"That's not what I meant…"

His nephew gives him a shove. "Just get up there."

Charlie toils up the embankment to join the others assembled behind the crash barrier. And there, he freezes because, after seeing the rest of the town so changed, this place is exactly the same. Two lanes of dual carriageway, the central reservation, two more lanes in the other direction and then you're safe. It doesn't look far, but it's deceptive because it only runs straight for half a mile in either direction, and there are thick overhangs of broom and bramble obscuring the view. You just have to chance it and hope you won't find a truck topping eighty bearing down on you before you even reach the median. As if summoned, headlights swing into view and seconds later a white van barrels past, the dirty logo on the side blurred. The bushes shake in its wake.

A confusion of grainy images and stern warnings blossom in Charlie's memory.

*Look left, look right. Always remember the Green Cross Code. A mother, hand over her mouth as if to cage, too late, the child who has just run out between parked cars.*

"Stop," Charlie says. As a kid, those little one minute films had terrified him. As an alternative comedian he'd torn them down with ridicule, but it's gone full circle now. He blinks the memories away, but the itchy fear lingers. "Just…wait a minute." They all look at him, Lesley and Gary glowering, Keli grinning even as another vehicle blazes past, causing her hair to whip across her gleeful face, Eric reserved as ever. "This *won't* work. Even if I go through with this, I've got nothing to offer."

After a long beat Lesley says, "Haven't you?"

And, finally, the penny drops. They mean *him*?

Whatever the objective *reality* of it, it is crystal clear now that his family not only believe in power of the Golden Path. They *need* it. And they don't just think that because he completed the five trials before that he can do it again. They somehow expect him to offer *himself* at the end too. Because Charlie – and you can forget all of the star status bullshit – is an outsider. Disposable. As panic bubbles up inside him, his eyes dart this way, that way, working out the best direction in which to make a break for it, but who is he kidding? He's a fifty-three year old borderline alcoholic and that Gary's a fit-looking lad. And besides, if they do have Raisa, she's not just bait. She's their back-up plan too.

It's getting harder and harder to fight against their conviction. The longer he's here in this place, with them, the less real everything else feels.

"Right," he says shakily, seeing it all laid out now. He's out of options.

Lesley arches an eyebrow, waiting.

"If I do this…" He stops himself. The thing he never told anyone after he ran the Path was that the trials themselves hadn't actually been all that hard for the most part. Frightening, yes, but far from impossible if you just brazened through. At least, that was how it had seemed in retrospect. He'd been young, pumped up and – thanks to a lifetime of his mother's words of wisdom – absolutely convinced that he was claiming his birth right. In the years since, he'd rationalised that he just got incredibly fucking lucky that day. Favoured by sheer fluke, in a way that Eric and Andrew and who knows how many others were not.

He can see now how that might seem to true believers. They think he's *charmed*.

This is insane. All of it. But he has no choice now.

"If I do this," he says. "You need to promise me that Raisa will be all right. You'll let her go."

"And have her run to the filth?" Keli scoffs. "Fuck off."

But Lesley pulls rank. "Soon as it's done, we'll let her go," she says. "But you'll need to be quick about it. If you get my meaning."

It's bluster. An extra layer of threat that is completely unnecessary by this point, just laid on for the fun of it. Keli and Gary are even laughing.

"You've got me now," Charlie says. "That's what you wanted. You don't need her, so promise me you'll let her go."

"You're just wasting time now," Gary sneers. "*Uncle*."

Charlie has vague fluttering thoughts of holding out at the Tombs until he can effect some sort of escape with Raisa, but he can't make them keep still long enough to work out how. He'll have time to think, he tells himself, once he's on the Path.

The next words he speaks, he realises, commit him. "So, what's the ask?"

There is always an offer. And there is always an ask.

"You'll know when the time comes," Lesley says, making it plain that's the last word on the matter.

Two cars speed past on the road, side by side like they're racing.

"All right." Charlie takes a deep breath that doesn't steady him like he hoped it would, then clambers clumsily over the barrier and then stands there, gripping the cold metal hard.

He remembers the words.

*The Road must be crossed without fear or care.*
*Don't look left, don't look right. Don't look at all.*

He closes his eyes. And walks.

As soon as he is moving, the memory of the last time rushes back. He remembers the road fumes. The summer breeze on his cheek. The weight of the old green Adidas bag slung over his shoulder, and the panicked scrabbling inside it. He remembers fizzing with a cocktail of fear and righteous excitement. And he remembers working out some sort of logic to the trial. You don't run or try and dodge. You just put one foot in front of the other foot like you're strolling down to the corner shop for your mum's fags. It isn't even that far.

And so that's what he does. His ears want to listen, his feet want to warn him of coming thrumming vibrations, but he ignores them and keeps walking, and before he knows it his shin connects with the central barrier. Easy as that. It's only when he lets out a long, shuddering breath that he realises that he'd been holding it all the way over.

He could open his eyes now, look back and reassure himself that the others know he means to go through with this, but that wasn't what he did the last time and he's suddenly convinced that he needs to replicate the last time as closely as possible. It's illogical, but he never truly freed himself from superstition, did he? No amount of therapy will ever unpick all of those tangles. So, he keeps his eyes closed and he presses on.

The central barrier is actually two, back to back, and he has to stretch to straddle them. Feeling the metal scrape the inside of his trailing leg, he worries about the state his good suit is going to end up in, but quickly banishes that ridiculous thought as irrelevant.

The central reservation is grassy and uneven. Edging forward, he searches for the asphalt and ends up catching it with his toe, pitching forward, hauling himself back. *Fuck, fuck.* Off balance, his adrenaline spikes and he's unable to prevent himself from breaking into a run. He's three, four strides into it when he feels the thunder coming from his left. His eyelids fly open. He's almost reached the first white line but he's not going to make it all the way across before the supermarket delivery truck coming up on the inside lane. Worse, a cobalt blue Audi has pulled out to overtake, and is also heading right for him. There's nowhere for him to go. Twin horns scream out in discord and then several tons of hurtling machinery is upon him. And, just as quickly, is gone.

There's a burning smell, and Charlie spots the arc of black tyre rubber the truck left during the last second swerve into the breakdown lane that is very possibly the only reason it's not him who is smeared across the road.

The realisation that it's *not* going to be the same as last time shocks him. But deep down he already knew that would be the case, didn't he? Because he's not the same naively entitled little shit that he was back then either. This is going to be a whole new adventure.

Charlie forces his legs into motion and half jogs, half staggers the remaining distance. Climbing over the last barrier, he discovers the slope on this side of the road is treacherous and his fancy shoes are useless when he begins to slip. He grabs for the bushes but misses, tumbles, hitting every rock and lumpy sod on the way to the bottom. He lies still in long grass, trying to catch his breath and feeling groundwater seep into the seat of his trousers.

When he finally feels able to sit up, daisies and dandelions are crowding around him. He's properly on the Path now.

# The Lightning Factory

Charlie dusts himself down, though there's little he can do about the mud on his jacket and trousers or the gravel scuffs on his shoes. A meadow of waving grass stretches out before him, the season's last wildflowers offering spots of colour. Bluebells and cornflowers, wanton poppies and tall spears of foxglove. No gold that way, though. The dandelions and daisies lead off to the left, following the meadow's northern perimeter.

So, that's the way he goes. *Like to like, weed to weed.*

Soon there are drooping buttercups among the flowers peeking out of the grass, delicate St John's Wort too, leading the way to another slope, this one diving down into a railway cutting. The bank is choked with gorse bushes and, though their season should be past by now, these too are in bloom. Their tiny cuplike blossoms glimmer golden and the scent of honeyed coconut swims around Charlie as he forces a path downwards. The thorns are vindictive, and his fingers and palms are thoroughly scratched by the time he reaches the bottom.

The railway line is an old goods route, the sort that run through the silent parts of towns largely without the knowledge of those who live and work nearby. The sleepers and shale are black, the metal rust brown, with only the bright upper surfaces of the rails themselves indicating that the line is in use. The railway isn't one of the trials, though. Charlie just has to follow it for a bit, but that doesn't mean there's no danger. The clusters of gorse blossom meander from one side of the track to the other. To follow the Path faithfully you have to cross over and back several times, and the trains come up from behind you thunderingly fast. He remembers the horrible anticipation each time he had to pick his way across the rails. One very close call had been the first occasion his teenage cockiness had been tested. The possibility worming its way in that he wasn't as special as he believed himself to be. If he was killed down here no one would ever know, and the comedy career he was so convinced he was *fucking made for* would never come to pass. This time it's worse. A lifetime of experience has robbed him of that confidence, and it's not only his own life that's at stake. Every step he takes now is fraught with anxiety.

At this moment though, the track is dormant. As he walks alongside it, loose stones skitter away from his shoes, loud in the silence that is not quite a silence. The high voltage line, suspended above him by gantries spaced along the track like skeletal giants, hums. It's the kind of noise that you don't hear so much as feel in the sutures of your skull, and it's getting louder. Charlie walks on until the gorse flowers run out on his side then, without looking behind him, quickly crosses first one rail, then the other.

It's getting dark now. Chilly too. Up in the wider world, the last of blue in the sky is turning peach as a late summer sunset settles in, but down here it's already as murky as October. Only the yellow blossoms brighten the way.

By the time Charlie crosses back over again, the electrical noise has become a chorusing thrum and the air has taken on a greasy feel that makes him want to rub his hands, though he's irrationally afraid that doing so will cause sparks. His teeth have started to ache.

This is madness. He shouldn't have come back. Shouldn't have obeyed that vestigial sense of... what was it? Decency? Duty? Whatever it was, they'd expected it of him. He remembers Lesley at the crematorium. *Cutting it fine there, weren't you?* she'd said without an ounce of surprise. He was that predictable, and they'd just been waiting to take advantage.

Raisa *had* been the surprise. A gift, even. *Fuck.* He wonders who did the deed. Tricked her with some plausible lie, forced her into a car and spirited her away. Gary looks like he's no stranger to that kind of work. He's got the same energy as the Stella-fuelled thugs that latched themselves onto football in the nineties. Charlie'd got a whole European tour out of playing up to those arseholes. They'd flocked to see him, spaffed thousands on his shitty, borderline-fascist merch. When, from time to time, it turns up on eBay, it makes him sick. He wonders if that tour was him at his absolute worst. It's hard to say, there's been a lot of competition.

He shoves his hands in his pockets and presses on. He shouldn't be dwelling on that shit. He should be planning what he's going to do when he makes it to the end of the Path. He half considers maybe trying to catch an animal as an alternative offer...but what does he know about trapping animals? That first time, he'd had enough trouble grabbing a cat who knew him well enough to come mooching for a greasy bit of doped fried chicken. A wild animal? No chance.

And even if there was some conveniently lame rabbit or badger just waiting out here for him to stumble over, it wouldn't be enough. Not according to Lesley.

*How much of a future would you have got for a cat?* she'd said.

Suddenly, vividly, he remembers the foxes. As much as he *tried* to forget what happened down here, he never really had. Moments have flashed sporadically into his thoughts countless times over the years, fired by any number of unexpected associations. But the encounter with the foxes he'd forgotten entirely until now. He'd been on this stretch when the furious bumping of the Adidas bag against his shoulder had suddenly stilled. It had taken him a moment to see the reason: a mother fox and two kits sitting among the bushes on the other side of the tracks, alertly watching his progress. They'd stared at each other, sharing a moment of communion. Then the mother had issued a sharp bark that might have been encouragement or a challenge or a warning but, before Charlie could work out which, the moment had been shattered in bone-rattling fashion by a train. When it had passed, the foxes were gone.

Another reason to leave the animals be. They're part of this place.

The bag had remained so still that Charlie'd wondered if the fleabag inside had died of fright given its initial state of decrepitude. He'd begun to panic because he knew the offer needed to be alive but, just when he was working himself up to take a cautious peek, a long, low, rolling growl had issued from inside. And though it put his mind at rest that he still had something to offer, it'd unnerved the bejesus out of him too.

All of that had been just before he came to the kite. And here – as on a rewound video tape – it is again in exactly the same spot, a diamond of old blue polythene snagged in the last of the gorse bushes. Its long red streamer tail and white strings flutter restlessly, although the air is absolutely still. Above, the powerlines are droning now in fits and bursts like broken loudspeakers.

Beyond the gorse, the track curves away to the right, and a hundred yards further on it'll enter a tunnel. Before that, however, there's The Lightning Factory. Charlie doesn't know who came up with that name for this towering fortification illuminated in shivering floodlight, but – approaching it now with the kite in his hand – he thinks it's apt. The humming emanates from it in queasy pulses. The yellow Danger signs on the chain link fence rattle in sympathy.

Around the other side of the Factory, he'll find a locked steel door set into the slope. Charlie can see the key for that door balanced on a ledge just below a ceramic insulator stack near the top of one of the transformer towers where the power goes out to the overhead line.

*At the Factory, dare to fly*, he remembers. *Defy the lightning in the sky.*

In other words, you need the key to continue along the Path. The idea is to knock it off with the kite, but last time he hadn't even bothered with that, just vaulted the fence and started climbing. *Easy*, he'd thought. *So easy.* It was only when he'd found himself reaching up, stretching, his fingers almost brushing the key, and it had occurred to him how exactly his pose had mimicked that one public information film with the kid trying to get his frisbee back, that he'd even thought about the danger. And he'd laughed, thinking about the film's almost comical ending: a grimace of shock and flared jeans set on fire like something from a Hammer film. Laughing again because he wasn't a loser like that kid had been, he'd reached further, toppled the key to the ground and jumped down after it, stopping only to retrieve the Adidas bag before heading off to the next station. *Easy.*

He remembers almost running in his eagerness to unlock the gate. Buzzing, as if the Lightning Factory had powered him up like the Duracell bunny.

Now Charlie's here again, that memory feels like a tall tale someone's told, so outrageous that everyone knows they're not expected to believe it. He can feel the power rolling off the Factory in dreadful waves. There's no way he's getting any closer to it than he absolutely has to. So, it'll have to be the kite.

Charlie tries to direct his thoughts away from the memory of that *other* cautionary film about playing near electricity, the one very specifically about the kite and the pylons, but he fails. He remembers the oblivious lad, the rising kite, the inevitable *flashbang* so clearly that it feels like a premonition. Fear grips his spine like a cold fist and, he realises, this is probably the way you were *supposed* to feel watching those little government funded warnings as a kid. Hell, if you grew up with the absolute knowledge that fooling around in these sorts of places would kill you, you'd avoid them like the plague, wouldn't you?

He hasn't got a choice now, though. If he doesn't do this someone else will, and they'll bring Raisa along for the ride.

The kite squirms in his grip as if impatient to be let loose, so Charlie takes a deep breath and lets it go.

For a second or two, the kite bobs in the air front of him, then shoots upwards, straight for the humming powerlines. He yanks at the nylon strings, fumbling one of them as, instead of ducking obediently back towards him, the kite loops hard to the right. Scrambling, he manages to gather the errant string and get the kite back under a short rein a dozen feet above his head. The plastic bellies and strains as if in an increasingly stiff breeze. It's getting harder with each passing second to keep it under control. He needs to get this done.

Little by little, Charlie's fingers remember the fine movements required to get the kite to go where he wants. The rhythm of twitches and pulls. And for a few minutes it's like he really is a kid again, playing the kite, guiding it higher, and again a little higher. With every inch closer to the key, however, he can feel the pull of the non-existent wind becoming stronger and more capricious, the kite's tail switching like that of an angry cat. Charlie's arm muscles are starting to burn from the effort and his face is itchy with sweat, but he can't do anything about that. He needs both hands and all of his concentration. He plays it out another few inches and the nose of the kite rises level with the insulator. So close. He lets it out a little more, but this time it doesn't rise. He tugs, cajoles. The kite drops, the strings slacken, and he's been fighting the pull so long he's momentary taken aback. Caught out when the kite suddenly soars upwards, Charlie pulls to the left, yanks hard right, but he's not going to be able to stop it hitting the lines.

He lets go of the strings.

There's an explosion of light and he's knocked back like a bus has hit him. He can smell a greasy burning and his head is ringing, but it's only when he slowly sits up that he becomes aware of the pounding pain from the flash burn glistening across his right palm. The longer he stares at it, the fiercer the pain becomes. With his other hand he reaches into his inside pocket and fishes out the packet of Ibuprofen he keeps on hand for hangover emergencies. Just two left. He chokes both of them down, and then looks for the kite. The only evidence that there had ever been one is something black melted over the fence and a flaccid stump of red tail.

They key, though? It's no longer on the ledge. Charlie scans for it, finally spotting it on the ground at the foot of the transformer. Tantalising close, but... *Fuck*. How is he going to get over there one-handed?

"Alright, Uncle Charlie? Haven't you been a lucky boy?"

Charlie twists around to see Gary and Eric approaching along the tracks. It's Eric who spoke. He's still carrying Summer. Her little arms are draped around his neck, head nestled into the crook of his shoulder, and despite all the drama she appears to be sleeping.

Eric tilts his head, displaying his facial scars to the harsh light. "Course you know that I wasn't quite so fortunate here."

"Though, if you hadn't let go of that string in time..." Gary chips in. Grinning, he mimes a line shooting across his chest from one side to another and then his heart exploding. "Epic fail, mate. Lucky boy, indeed."

Eric reaches down to take Charlie's good hand and pull him to his feet.

"What are you doing here?" Charlie says.

"We're here to help, of course," Eric replies.

"Make sure the job gets done," Gary adds antagonistically as he turns his attention to the Lightning Factory. "So near and yet so far, eh? Fucking old spaz."

Gary looks pleased to be able to say openly what he's obviously been thinking all day. More than that, Charlie thinks as he watches his nephew drop his jacket on the ground and roll up his shirt sleeves, there's a punchy sort of glee about him. As if he believes this should have been his job all along. His birth right. Which raises the question…if his father and his younger brother both tried and failed to run the Path, why has there been no mention of him doing the same? Gary takes two fistfuls of chain link and hauls himself up the fence. Landing on the other side, he scoops up the key and brandishes it with a triumphant grin to demonstrate that its retrieval had been the easiest thing in the world.

"I don't get it," Charlie says, accepting a clean white handkerchief from Eric and closing his hand gingerly around it. The soft cotton is a relief and the painkillers are starting to kick in as well. He's grateful, but he can't understand how the lads following him here improves the situation.

"You never have," Eric says quietly as they watch Gary swagger back over to them. The words are almost inaudible against the electricity's hungry pulse.

"What do you mean?" Charlie says, but neither brother deigns to answer.

Summer wriggles in her dad's arms and whines sleepily. Eric snugs the collar of her blue anorak around her little neck. "Come on," he says. "This is taking too long."

# The Lake

Behind the steel door is a stairwell. On his previous visit, Charlie was too hyped up by his successes to pay much attention, but this time he finds the descent unsettling oppressive. The lamps bolted to the wall are dim and too far apart. The air is dank and filled with echoes that Charlie is reluctant to add to even with so many questions bubbling on his lips. The Path is supposed to be a personal risk to be undertaken and rewarded. A contract with the fates, the fears, the...monsters. Whatever *they* actually are that reside in the dene. He recalls his mum's words again: *You have to walk The Golden Path, son, if you want your due.* Other people being here can only fuck that up. Can't they? Then he thinks about Lesley's claim that she'd followed him and brought Edward Pettifer with her. And how he hadn't believed her.

He catches himself. Tries to remind himself, as has been doing for years, that *none of this is any more than childish dares in the woods.* That any significance was solely due to his mum's crazy old lies woven through a jumble of half remembered folk tales and communal fears. But it's too late for that. At some point he's crossed the line of credibility and here he is, with his hand throbbing and his heart banging away in his chest. Although he'd tried so hard to forget it all, to rationalise it as damaging fantasy, the Path so far has been exactly the same as it was the last time. Easy? How had he imagined it was *easy*? With every step, with every station, with every dark bloom of memory, the fantastical has become credible again, the danger absolutely real. And there is much worse to come.

So, he keeps his mouth shut and follows the others down into the dark. Listens to the solid tread of three pairs of men's shoes. Step, step. Step, step. Step, step.

*Step, step?*

No. It's his imagination. A trick of the echoes. There's no one else in here, following them down with unshod, padding feet.

Quickening his pace, Charlie catches up with his nephews just as Gary is opening another door at the bottom. If it was getting dark before, it is full night down here in the dene. They emerge from a near vertical bank that towers above them, studded with boulders and slate shelves interspersed with sparse bushes. Ahead, stretches the floor of a narrow gorge. Its trees – towering oak bullying spindly birch, ash and holly fighting for the same patch of mossy, root-ridged ground – are animatedly frozen, like children playing *What's The Time Mister Wolf*. As if they'd been creeping up, about to pounce, before he looked at them. Charlie can see all of this because far above their heads are swatches of stars and moonlight diffused through shifting layers of cloud. Just enough light to see the crawling ground mist and, through it, the trail of flowers leading off through the trees like the Yellow Brick fucking Road.

It isn't the dene's darkness that blossoms in Charlie's memory now, however. It's the silence, thick as sodden cloth. Last time, after the exhilaration of the Lightning Factory, Charlie had been so unsettled here that he'd almost turned around and quit. It's just as bad now and he can see from the lads' faces that they're feeling it too. Summer's also begun to grizzle and won't be placated.

"Fucking hell," Gary mumbles. He chews his lip, then says again, louder, "*Fucking hell.*" His loutish arrogance has been punctured like a balloon, leaving a glassy fragility in his eyes. When Charlie thinks about lads like Gary he's known down the years, this isn't that much of a surprise.

"Come on," Eric says again. Charlie detects an edge of irritation in his voice as they both watch Gary stomping ahead, crushing the yellow blossoms of the Path underfoot as if he doesn't even know they're there. He's mumbling to himself too, though whatever he has to say is smothered by the strange acoustics of the dene.

Eric shifts Summer from the crook of one arm to the other. She's snuffling into his collar, a trail of snot bright on his lapel. With his usual stoicism he strides after his brother.

"Gary's afraid," Charlie says to Eric's back as he hurries to keep up.

"We're all afraid," says Eric. "That's the whole point." He pushes aside a branch. The dry, brown leaves whisper as they swing back.

"True enough," Charlie replies. "But it's more than that, isn't it? His whole family have tried to do this. His father, his wee brother…"

"Mum too." Eric nods reluctantly. "More than once."

"And yet he's the eldest son. Must be a lot of pressure on him."

Eric steps on a mossy twig that snaps clean in half but makes only the softest of sounds. "Maybe. Who knows what goes on in someone else's head, eh?"

"Eric..." Charlie grabs his nephew's arm, yanks him around.

"*What?*" Eric's face is blanched by starlight. Only his cheeks sport spots of colour. They look like lichenous growths.

"What are you doing here?" Charlie says. "This isn't how it's meant to work. It's supposed to be—"

"All about you?" Eric's expression is so scornful there's no doubting he's Lesley's son. "But it's not. It never was. It's about the community. A deal with *them* on behalf of all of us. For custodianship of the Land." He scowls at Charlie's incomprehension. "Look, whatever you thought of Nanna, she understood people. How to get the best out of them. Mate, she'd pegged you as a narcissist since you were first able to say *me, me, me.* So, she fed that in you. Nurtured it until you were dead set on following the Path to achieve your own pathetic dream. She'd no way of knowing you'd actually manage it. It was a punt and a hope like they all are, but you got lucky. Your stars were right, or whatever, and you got what you wanted. But that was only part of it. It was Mum following on who did the hard bit on behalf of the rest of us who were going to actually live our lives here."

Eric's tirade hits Charlie like a gut punch. *My little star,* Brenda used to call him, still laughing at whatever cheeky quip he'd come out with. *You ought to be on the stage.* Could she really have been setting him up for the dangers of the Path, even at that age? Had risking the life of her son been an acceptable gamble for her? He can't honestly say he finds it hard to believe.

"For the good of the community?" The words trip quietly from his lips.

"Yeah, for the community. For the Land. Our Land."

Eric's obviously eager to be on his way again, but Charlie holds his gaze. "And yet here I am," he says. "An outsider."

Eric looks away. "Yeah, here you fucking are." From ahead there comes a faint splash. Eric grimaces and then they're off again, Charlie hustling to keep up with the lad's long stride. Before he knows it they're at the water's edge.

The Lake is a slovenly, secretive body of water, its margins rendered ambiguous by drunken trees and thickets of reeds. The darkling waters lick and lap in a quietly sibilant language. Promising, enticing. Drawing you near. Charlie's skin shrinks in a whole-body shiver of fear as another black flower blossoms…and he remembers – *linger by the lake as long as you dare, tiptoe past what's hiding there* – the sudden shadow looming in the corner of his vision, the heavy blow between his shoulders that had sent him sprawling in the shallows. It had gripped the back of his head, held him down. He'd struggled, he'd thrashed. He'd stolen gasps of air between gulps of rancid water. Throughout his ordeal he'd pictured his assailant as tall, black robed and faceless. Just like the figure from the public information film warning kids not to play near ponds. *The Spirit of Dark and Lonely Water.* By the time Charlie had been ready to chance the Path he'd seen enough proper horror movies that a cowled figure should have been a cliché, but that little film, slipped in between the after-school cartoons like a razorblade among your

Hallowe'en sweeties, had cut him deeply. Charlie was never more terrified than in those minutes spent writhing in the water. Knowing that, for all his self-confidence, there was a force far stronger than he was down here, and there was nothing he could do about it.

But then there had been a noise, sharp and quickly stifled. He'd thought later it had sounded like a fox's bark, though there was no evidence of one when he'd recovered enough to look around. Nor was there any robed figure. There was just himself, soaked and shivering in the shallows. Permitted to continue. At the time, he'd taken it as another sign. He wouldn't have used words like *fate* or *destiny*, merely that he was, after all, entitled to his due. He guesses his stars had been right, or whatever. Maybe there's something in what Eric said after all.

Standing here among the reeds now, he can't prevent himself from casting around for the awful presence coming back to finish the job.

"Gary?" Eric is only a few feet away, but it sounds like he's shouting into a pillow. "Gaz?"

Summer is squirming in his grip now, red faced and bawling. "Daaaaddy."

From their left comes more splashing. And Gary's voice too, yelling inchoately for the most part but with sporadic moments of clarity like bubbles popping in the murk. "See them… Look, *fucking look*… So many of them… Coming here… Coming *here*… Drowning's too good… Fucking…" *Splash.* "Fucking get them…" *Splash, splash.*

It sounds like Gary's found his own fears to battle. Whatever he's doing, though, he's properly off the path now.

The notion of willingly going into that water gives Charlie the absolute fear, but Eric starts in the direction of the noise, only for Summer to choose that moment to wriggle completely out of his arms. "Want Daddy," the tot screams as Eric awkwardly half catches her, half lowers her to the ground. "*Daaaaddy.*"

As Summer totters determinedly away on her stubby little legs, Eric is torn between trying to recapture her and going to help his brother. His indecision is resolved by another, increasingly desperate, bout of shouting.

"Get her under control, will you?" he growls at Charlie. "And whatever it is you need to do here, do it quickly." Then he's charging off through the bushes.

As soon as Eric is out of sight, Summer slows and looks around, flapping her arms in distress. She sits abruptly down on the ground and begins to cry again. Charlie never settled down with anyone long enough to have kids, and having to deal with shit like this is one of many skills that've passed him by. So he's surprised to find that there might be a sliver of paternalism in his DNA after all.

"Hey, Summer," he says, crouching. "It's me. Your Uncle Charlie."

The teary glare that comes his way strikes him for some reason as the first time she's *really* looked at him. There's bewilderment in that look. There's fear, and there's hope. It's almost as if she's been half asleep all day.

"Where's my Daddy?" she asks in a tiny voice, and Charlie knows with sudden certainty that she does not mean Eric.

"Come here, mate," he says as gently as he can. "We'll find your Daddy." She allows herself to be scooped up. Her little body is warm. He can feel her heart beating.

Juggling Summer to minimise the weight on his injured arm, Charlie makes his way cautiously around the reeds. They grow thick as hedges here, but there's a slender rabbit run between them that leads down to where the lake comes right up to the trees. The roots are submerged and there's no way of going around, but it's only about fifteen feet wide here. It might be jumpable if the path offered you a run-up, but it doesn't. What you need to do – *tiptoe* – is make stepping stones.

As Charlie sits Summer down and starts hunting among the rushes – quickly coming up with a log, a flat rock, another rock – he pushes from his mind any desire to imagine what might be happening to Gary right now. Whatever it is, Charlie finds it hard to scrape together much in the way of sympathy.

Stretching out, Charlie places the log gently into the water then, picking up the bigger of the two rocks, he steps onto the log. It wobbles but settles. Again, he stretches, dropping the rock mid-channel, snatching his hand back from the splash. He hops back to the shore, smiles at Summer, who is watching him with clear, wide eyes, and repeats the process with the last rock. This one settles just below the surface. *Shit*. It'll have to do though.

When he goes back to scoop up the kid, he realises that it's gone very quiet around the lake.

Charlie finds Eric a little further on, hunkered at the water's edge. His trousers are soaked up to the knees and there is something darkening his shirt and his hands. There's no sign of Gary, but Eric is looking out over the settling waters. There are shapes out there. Beyond the geometric angles of a shopping trolley, there's a darker patch just below the surface that might be pondweed, or a weighed down bin bag, or...

"Where's your brother?" Charlie stares fixedly at his nephew's ashen face.

"Gone," Eric says.

"Well, I suppose he's done his bit," Charlie says bitterly. The words *for the community* dangle unspoken.

Eric turns to stare at him for a long, unblinking moment. Eventually, he says: "I just don't get it. What makes you so special?"

"What do you mean?"

"What do I mean?" Eric drags his fingers through his hair, then slowly stands up. "Look at you. You're a middle-aged hasbeen with no beliefs or convictions. You don't give a shit about your family, your people, your country. You're...*nothing*. But they let you succeed where so many worthier people failed. Seriously, mate. What is so fucking special about you?"

Charlie has no answer for that, and Eric doesn't seem to expect one. His nephew shrugs, as if to dislodge the inertia, then reaches out.

"We've got to get this finished. Give me the kid."

Summer's arms tighten around Charlie's neck.

"I don't think she wants that," he says, astounded by how level his own voice is. "She just wants her Dad."

Eric deliberates, stony-faced. "Fine," he mutters. "She weighs a fucking ton anyway." Shoving his hands in his pockets, he stomps off following the trail of flowers along the shoreline. "Just remember," he calls over his shoulder, the words attenuated to an almost whisper, "your girlfriend's depending on you, so you'd better do your bit too."

Charlie follows his nephew around the edge of the Lake. The black water is calmer now, watchful, and he's disinclined to speak again until the Path leads them away from the shore, back in among the trees. The ground under their feet becomes firmer, the air clearer, and Charlie's ears normalise with an audible pop. He can hear the soft impact of his shoes on the loam again. He can hear Eric cursing to himself, and every light lungful of Summer's breath.

Charlie catches up when Eric comes to an uncertain halt. "You're right." He adjusts his hold on the little girl again. "She's heavier than she looks." And she is, he tells himself, but she's not a burden.

"Yeah." Eric scowls in indecision, although the Path is as bright as it's always been. After a moment he sets off again, noticeably to the left of the trail of flowers but close enough that Charlie doesn't have to leave the Path himself as he follows on.

"So, who are her real parents?" he says. Eric doesn't respond beyond a stiffening of his shoulders. "I mean it hardly matters now, does it?"

Gruffly, Eric says, "Like you say, it doesn't matter."

"Okay, but, if I'm part of this," Charlie says, "if we're really doing this together for the community, I want to know."

"Well, that's too bad because I don't fucking know, do I Charlie?" Eric's outburst ricochets around the trees, scattering fragments of emotion like shreds of bark and leaf. Charlie hears anger and fear in it mostly, but there's guilt too. Guilt and shame. "Kel pinched her off some gypos at a Sunday market down in Brum. They've got so many brats they probably didn't even notice. Fuck it, mate, nobody cares anyway.

You seen any headlines about a nationwide manhunt? No? Exactly."

Yeah, there's shame all right. It burns underneath every word of the boy's bluster, consuming him from the inside. Fucking hell, you can justify it anyway you like but any even half-decent human being couldn't *not* feel shame given the task that this lad's been asked to do.

Is doing. Regardless.

And it's been a real team effort, hasn't it? Snatching this random child on the margins of society. Having a registered nurse on hand to drug the kid to stop her causing a fuss, and a kidnapped friend to ensure that the prodigal uncle plays his part. Right now, Charlie feels about as far from fucking favoured as you can get, but he thinks he's finally beginning to understand.

Lesley would have masterminded the running of it, but it has all the hallmarks of a Brenda plan. He's sure of that. If his mother had set him up the first time to lead the way for Lesley to bring poor Edward Pettifer to his doom, he has no doubt she'd quite readily have used her own incipient demise – the only event that might ever conceivably entice Charlie back here at all – as the springboard to go through it all again. To what end? He doesn't know. What's a pikey kid's life worth exactly?

Charlie tells himself he won't let it happen. That he'll think of something. But he said that about Raisa too and came up with nothing. And they're getting close to the end now.

Eric stops again. Though the trees grow tight together here, there's still room for the dandelions and daisies. In the dene's dark they are luminous, but it's clear that Eric can't see them. He's lost the Path, just like his brother did. "Which way now?" he says, spinning stupidly round.

"Down."

# The Stranger

Over his nephew's shoulder, Charlie sees movement. Just an infinitesimal twitch in the shadows, but enough to reveal to him a fox. The animal is the colour of earth and barely visible stretched out among the feet of an oak tree. Only the flick of its black-rimmed ears draws the eye, that and the golden eyes staring at Charlie, right into his heart, his soul. He glances back to Eric for just a second, and of course in that second, the fox has silently upped and gone.

*What makes you so special?*

Shaking his head, Charlie pushes by, taking the lead. Wending between the mossy boles, he picks a careful path among the roots that ridge the ground here like petrified veins, following the gradient, every step taking them downwards.

After a few more minutes, Eric says abruptly, "What's he like?"

"What's who like?"

"You know who." When Charlie doesn't answer, Eric goes on, his nervousness spilling over, and now he sounds like a scared kid. "Mum coached us through the other stations, but this one…she won't talk about this one. The Stranger. All she's ever said is *he's your own worst enemy.*"

Which explains why Lesley sent the boys instead of coming herself.

A final black flower slowly unfurls. The one Charlie's been dreading the most. Because Lesley is right.

"Your own worst enemy? That's one way of putting it," he says. Because that's the rhyme, isn't it? *Beware the Stranger in the Dene. His gifts are never as they seem.*

Charlie remembers what Lesley was like as a kid; keen and feisty, but still quite innocent in her own serious way. The Stranger she met when she followed her big brother into the woods with her credulous little friend in tow probably seemed like a thrilling secret to her. Charlie can only imagine what returning would be like for her, with all of the doubts and frailties that adulthood brings. That's even before you take into account the fact she's had the boy's murder on her conscience for thirty years.

He tries *not* to imagine what it will be like for himself. Tries not to picture that face, hear that voice. Concentrates on following the path. His feet – step, step – and Eric's – step, step – following behind.

Step, step. Step, step. Step, step.

*Pad, pad.*

His heart freezes. His feet take root. And he feels little Summer cling tighter than ever, trembling violently now, because she's looking over his shoulder and can see what's behind them.

"Rrrowlll," says the Cat. "Long time, no see, Chaaarlie." He does that awful chaotic hiccupping thing that Charlie knows of old to be laughter. "Until rrreeecently, anyway."

Charlie turns around and finds that Eric has vanished. In his nephew's place is a seven-foot-tall patchwork of roadkill fur. It has tabby stripes and tortoiseshell brindling, it is sooty black and snowy white and the colour of Old English marmalade, and where the fur has fallen victim to mange, crusty grey-pink skin shows through. Its limbs are oddly proportioned and wrongly jointed. It walks upright on two legs, has only a twitchy stump of a tail, and its claws flex with casual threat.

"No," Charlie says, knowing that the *recently* means Edinburgh, the funeral. Those had been lapses. Aberrations. "I didn't call on you. I didn't want you."

There's a fly buzzing around one of Cat's rheumy eyes. "You neeed me."

Charlie shakes his head. "That's not true."

When Cat laughs it shows its fat tongue and a rag of flesh snagged in its teeth. "Rrreallly? Look at you, standing heeere on the very spot where we first met and saying that with a strrraight face? Everything you are, you owe to meee, Chaaarlie. Without me: You. Are. Nothing."

Charlie takes a deep, shaking breath. "The world's moved on," he says. "The things I used to say aren't funny anymore. They never were. No one wants to hear them. I've got new stories to tell."

Cat stoops until his face is only inches from Charlie's. His whiskers sproing like bent piano wires. "Oh, such liiies. Your auuoowdience is still there." His breath is like rotten garbage. "They're just waiting for you to come back to them. They're tired of being told to shushhh, that their concerns don't matter, that they're third class citizenszz in their own land. All they neeed is a voice to unite them. One of their own. You know it's truuue."

Charlie does. Of course, they've never gone away. The family, the community. All the white, working class conservatives of Morsley. And hundreds of towns like it. The ones who say, *you can't joke about anything anymore.* And, *it's just a harmless bit of fun.* And they're correct; there are right things and wrong things to say these days. Sometimes, a comedian can say the wrong things. And when you're that kind of comedian, telling those sorts of jokes to people in the pubs, in the clubs, in the theatres, you see it in their faces. First the shock…then the relief at being allowed to laugh at something they've had to keep locked up. Because laughter is validation. Laughter is connection. The feeling of power that comes with uncorking that in a crowd is an *indescribable rush.* But Charlie is not that kind of comedian. Not anymore.

"No," he says, though his defiance feels paper thin. "It's not me."

Cat laughs again, all howls and vowels. "Who am I?"

"The Stranger," Charlie says leadenly.

"And who is that."

"My best friend and my own worst enemy."

"And who is *that.*"

"Myself," he whispers.

Cat grins a carrion grin. "Quite so."

"But I *don't want* it." Charlie takes a deliberate step away, holding Summer closer than ever. "I didn't ask for it. I was forced to come here against my will."

"And yet heeere you are, running straight for The Tombs with an offer in your arms." Cat shows tongue and teeth. "Actions speak looouwder than words, bucko."

"I'm not going to harm the girl," Charlie whispers.

"So, it's to be your friend instead?"

"No, I'm…"

"You're what?" Cat strokes Charlie's cheek with his paw. The damp, matted fur, the calloused pad. Charlie can't speak. "What you're going to do is carry on a little further down the hill and make the offer. They really want you to. You know that, don't you? You're an important part of their plan."

"What plan?" he hears himself whisper.

"Why the plan to restore the Land, of course!" Cat pulls a comic leer. "The traditions, the values. That's what they want most of all, and you will be rewarded for your part. Oh, they'll give your friends and family what they want too, but it's really all about you. That's why you're the only one who can see the Path all the way to the end." He unsheathes the tip of one claw and with horrible playfulness taps Charlie on the nose. "You'rrre the man."

Cat shoves Charlie hard and he stumbles, trips on something, a rock, a root, and lurches sideways. Summer cries out in fright and it's all Charlie can do not to drop her as his shoulder slams against a tree. The impact jars his shoulder joint and collar bone, and his injured hand is suddenly burning again too.

Cat has melted away.

Charlie sucks in a long moan of despair. He just wants this all to be over, but Cat's right. He's the man whether he likes it or not, and everyone knows there's no going back on the Golden Path. But... that's Charlie's mum talking, isn't it? That's his indoctrination. It doesn't mean it's *true*... Looking back the way he came, though, he sees that the trail of yellow flowers has withered and vanished, and with it so does his fleeting hope of escape. No, you can't go back. You can only follow the Path all the way to the end.

*You're the man.* The phrase sticks in his mind as he winds his way down through the crowding trees. *You're the man.* It sounds like *you're responsible, it's your fault.*

And in a way, he supposes, it is. It doesn't matter if Brenda had set it up. If he hadn't been so blindly, selfishly ambitious he'd have never dared to come here in the first place. Never succeeded in making his paltry offer and, by doing so, enabled little Lesley to make the community's much worse, much more meaningful one. It doesn't matter that he changed his mind later, that he turned away from the person he had been. Because he *had been* that person. He had been that greedy, that self-absorbed, that entitled.

*That special.*

What would he have said if his mum had told him the plan from the start? If he'd been told he could have the fame and notoriety, the adulation in the Mail, the editorial hit pieces in the Indie and the Guardian – which were every bit as good because it's all fucking column inches, isn't it? – but some nerdy little black kid wasn't going to be going home for his spaghetti hoops that night? He knows. He doesn't need Cat here to hook it out of him. He'd have shrugged and said, *well that's a shame, but sign me up.* Because that was the whole thing about growing up back then. Kids died. They got run over on the roads. They came a cropper playing near electricity or water. Constantly risked death or disfigurement fooling around with matches or fireworks, or in the kitchen while the chip pan was in full and furious bubble. And they went off into the woods with strangers too. It was on the news all the time. They were warned constantly. It was just a fact of life. So, yeah, he'd have taken that deal. Of course, he would.

And because he did, because he'd succeeded where few others ever had, he'd breathed real life into Brenda Mason's version of Morsley's dark little secret. Kept it alive and allowed it to evolve into something even nastier.

He's the fucking man, all right.

Charlie only realises he's crying when his vision blurs. He wipes his eyes with his sleeve but the tears keep coming, spilling down his cheeks and pattering down the back of Summer's anorak. As he stumbles onward, the gradient suddenly steepens and with a lurch he finds himself falling. There's a crunching agony in his ankles and knees when he hits the ground but somehow he manages again not to drop the kid or fall on top of her. He kicks something hollow and metallic, which rattles away from him. When he regains his breath and his vision clears, he recognises that it's a Tennent's Lager can. The can is folded in half, but you can still see the bikini-clad model with the big hair and pouty Page Three attitude. They haven't made those in decades.

This is it then. He's arrived.

# The Tombs

The Tombs is the deep, dark hole in the heart of the dene. It might have been a quarry once, but with its dramatic, towering, lushly overgrown walls, it strikes Charlie now that it must have been a local feature of significance for centuries before that. A place of pilgrimage in pagan times, perhaps. A site of damnation when the church took over.

What it's been for as long as Charlie has known of its existence is an illegal rubbish tip. You notice the cars first. Nearby there's a brown Austin Princess without wheels and a Morris Marina the colour of English mustard standing vertically, nose down, as if it had been driven straight down the cliff. Beyond them lies an old-style Mini flipped onto its roof, headlights smashed and windscreen pushed in as if under the pressure of a kid's careless thumb. Among the cars, the appliances. Old electric cookers with the grime burned-on around the rings. Chest freezers and twin tub washers, gaping maws filled with scummy water. Charlie sees a Rediffusion TV in a scroll-front wooden cabinet that did nothing to protect its screen from the fall, and beneath that the cracked orange carapace of a Flymo.

There are heaps, towers, drifts of junk piled on junk, an archaeology of obsolescence. Old things that the world no longer has a use for. And even though this is the deepest and darkest part of the dene, he can see it all because it is overgrown with flowers. Here there are thickets of blooming gorse and swathes of dandelions, daisies, buttercups and all manner of yellow blooms great and small. And they are brilliant, bathing the whole scene in a golden radiance that is neither gentle nor resplendent. It is terrifying.

And it's into that that Charlie must now go.

"It's all right." He gives the sobbing child a gentle pat. "It's going to be all right." But he doesn't move yet, because he knows that it's not going to be all right at all.

"What you doing waiting out here, you old arsehole?" Eric has appeared at the edge of the trees. From his flushed face and frantic eyes, Charlie guesses he found his own answer to his question about The Stranger. For Eric, it won't have been a seven-foot talking cat out of a series of children's safety animations who happens to share his name. For Eric, it'll be something different, although no less devastatingly persuasive. And there's no doubting it's had the required effect. The lad is bursting with frightened fury.

When Charlie's nephew jumps down, Summer starts whimpering again. A thin, mewling, "nooo".

"Come on!" Eric's bellow rebounds from the rocky walls. He gives Charlie a shove for good measure. "We've got to Get. This. Done."

With no choice but to do as he's bid, Charlie follows the flowers one last time. They lead him deep in among the piles of rubbish. Everywhere he looks his eye is snagged by the ephemera of his youth: the twisted foil wrapper from a tube of Spangles, a pair of Activision console paddle controllers and a spill of cartridges, a pogo stick snapped in half like a toothpick. He doesn't know why it is like this. To reconnect him to his thoughtless, selfish teenage self? There's no chance of that. He knows who he is.

And he knows now what he has to do.

While Eric stomps ahead, driven on by his own demons. Charlie hesitates for a just moment before following.

The unsettling, luminous path twists and spirals but it always leads downwards. Everything beyond the glow is in darkness. Charlie can't even see the stars anymore. There's an intensifying smell of lush verdure, overpoweringly earthy.

And then they reach the end. This is the place.

Five ancient fridges are arranged in a circle like standing stones. The colour of curdled cream, they are covered in dings and scratches and each has an old-fashioned steel clasp, the kind that means they can only be opened from the outside.

"Which one?" Eric goes from one ancient appliance to the next in frantic confusion.

"*Make your offer at the last,*" Charlie intones. "*Choose your coffer. Ask your ask.*"

"What?"

"Any of them. It doesn't matter."

"Right," Eric tugs the handle of the nearest. He seems surprised at the weight of it. "Bring her over."

"What's the ask?" Charlie says quietly.

"What?" Eric's expression twists into one of incredulity. "Are serious? You've not worked out Nanna's plan yet?" He shakes his head and turns to inspect the fridge's filthy interior.

In truth, Charlie doesn't care. He's doing it his way now. He's the man, after all.

"Hey, Eric? Did you hear the one about the bigot who walked into a bar?"

"*What?*"

Charlie's grip on the piece of pogo stick isn't what it could be, but he still gets plenty of heft into the blow. There's a dull clang and his nephew crumples. Dropping his weapon, Charlie lowers Summer gently to the ground, sitting her down among the flowers.

"It's going to be okay," he tells her again, and now he has made his decision he has some hope that it actually might be. For her at least.

He hesitates in front of the open fridge, looking down at Eric. There's a contusion on the back of his nephew's head but no blood, and he's pretty sure the lad will be all right when he comes to. For a moment he contemplates dragging Eric into the fridge, but instinct tells him that would not be an acceptable offer. They prefer the innocent and blameless. Eric's neither of those. Neither is Charlie, but he hopes *repentant* will do just as well.

Besides, Charlie's special. Charlie's the man. And even though Raisa thinks his new material is good and sharp and relevant, he's been kidding himself thinking that after all this time anyone out there might be even remotely interested in it.

He's finally accepted that he's finished.

Weird. He'd imagined that acknowledging that would feel like a relief, but he realises that part of him still rails against what he considers to be the injustice of it. Well, it's too late now. He climbs inside the fridge, pulling his knees up to his chest and bending his head down almost to meet them.

Charlie says, "Here is my offer and here is my ask. I want this kid to get back with her parents and live the rest of her life happy and untroubled. Not scared. Kids shouldn't grow up scared."

When he closes the door, he hears it latch with firm finality. The darkness is absolute. The only sound, his own breaths, loud and ragged, and his muscles are already starting to burn from his cramped posture. He'd thought he was calm but, now that there's no way back, he's skating around the rim of panic. *Fuck.* He thought he could make the sacrifice nobly, but he's too much of a coward, panting now, acutely aware that the faster he breathes the sooner his oxygen will be used up. *Fuckfuckfuck.* He needs to get out of here.

No. It has to happen this way. It's the *only* way.

He thinks of Summer, hopes to God Eric will take her back when he realises what Charlie has done.

He thinks of Raisa, hopes she'll be able to get on with her life now too. He's been a burden to her for far too long.

Charlie's breaths are getting shallow and he's starting to feel woozy. He shoves at the fridge door. It is absolutely solid. He yells, deafening himself, but keeps on yelling until he no longer has the air to do so. He knows for certain he's going to pass out, and the last feelings he's going to experience in this world are going to be pain and shame and everlasting regret.

The darkness is crushing. There's a stink of rotting garbage. A voice in his ear. "Oh, no, no, nooo," it says. "No escaping Nanna's plan."

When the door opens, he's not certain if his oxygen-starved brain is hallucinating or if he's getting the worst possible welcome to the afterlife. Either way the waxy, grey face that peers in at him is unmistakably that of Brenda Mason. She's wearing a stiff mortician's smile, but she's far from happy.

"Get the hell out of there, you," she croaks. "We're not done with you yet."

# Epilogue

*Facebook Group: Heart Of Britain*
*574k members  1350 posts today*

Bonfire of the Inanities – 5 November 2021

@HOB_admin: Here's Charlie Mason's epic Bonfire Night rant again. Keep sharing the video far and wide. Every time they take it down, we get stronger. They can't censor the fucking truth.

@truredwhiteandblu: They can't handle the truth! Comedy gold. Can't wait to see what he's got for us on the livestream tonight.

@Albion_defender: Man's a fucking legend. He really is. I'm sharing the fuck out of this. Everywhere.

---

Charlie's not exactly a prisoner. It's just that he can imagine nowhere else that would have him now. London's right out, that's for sure. And, honestly? It's not like he even misses it that much.

He wants to call Raisa, but he doesn't know what he'd say to her. He's relieved at least to know his family had been bullshitting about her all along. She'd fucked off back to London so fast after the funeral that she'd not even noticed her phone had been nicked until she was half-way home.

Summer, on the other hand? Well, no one talks about Summer. An offer was made and accepted. An ask granted. That's all that matters to them.

And already it seems to be working. A new DIY chain has opened up outlets throughout the Midlands and their main distribution centre is only a few miles outside of Morsley. The car plant has reopened too, only they're going to be making something called SMRs, which Charlie understands to be to do with the nuclear power industry, which has come back into favour as the country lurches belatedly away from its reliance on imported Russian gas. And the people of Chilwell have started clearing up the estate. Opening up the derelict houses, giving everything a lick of paint and an air of optimism. Taking defiant pride in their home. Reclaiming it. Their Land.

No one says out loud who's behind it. But everybody knows.

There's a knock on the car window. It's that tall lad, Steven. One of Eric's mates apparently, though Charlie hasn't seen Eric in some weeks. The family's been keeping their distance.

"You all set, Charlie?" Steven's voice is muffled both by the glass and the thick scarf he's wearing. He claps his gloved hands together for warmth.

Charlie doesn't want to go out into the bitter November cold, but *this is the gig*, right? Nodding, he switches off the engine and emerges from the vehicle.

"Brilliant," Steven says. He's a nice guy, Steven. He says *brilliant* a lot. Although not as much as he likes to repeat the range of inventive slurs he's picked up since getting involved in Heart Of Britain. It's not that he hates the *dracs* and the *cleaning ladies* more than any others, it's just that finds those terms the funniest. And loves having the licence to utter them aloud.

"So, we've got the bonfire started, as you can see, mate." Charlie's been trying to ignore it. Not so much the pyre itself but the stuffed guy on top clinging to a passable approximation of a raft. "And we've got a good wee crowd for you too," Steven goes on, indicating a cluster of warmly dressed people a distance from the crackling, spitting flames. Maybe twenty or thirty of them, adults and kids. There are lots of smiles. Someone takes out a box of matches – *shake, shake, shake* – lights a sparkler and gives it to a little girl who grins in wide-eyed delight as she starts to draw shapes in the freezing air.

Charlie's initial reaction is automatic. *Kids shouldn't play with sparklers*. His second is how much she resembles poor Summer.

There's a smattering of gloved applause, and even a few whoops, as he and Steven approach and take up position between the bonfire and the audience. Then the phones come out, the camera lights illuminating. Charlie feels sick. He always feels sick.

Steven is checking his tablet. "Ready to go live in thirty seconds." Then he laughs. "Man, the audience is massive."

Charlie closes his eyes. "How many?"

"Twenty-seven thou, no, twenty-eight now. And the comments are off the charts already." Steven grins. "Ready?"

"Twenty-eight thoousand," says Cat at Charlie's shoulder. "Hate to say I toold you so, but that's a lot of love, Charlie."

It is. And it's all for him. The part of him that wishes it wasn't feels impossibly distant right now.

Charlie grins too. He doesn't know if it's a real grin or a fake one, but that's showbusiness, isn't it? This is the only gig he's got. Through the tablet's little speakers he can hear the applause.

He just wishes he didn't love it so much.

# THE THREE BOOKS

*by*

## Paul StJohn Mackintosh

"I've been told that this is the most elegant thing I've ever written. I can't think how such a dark brew of motifs came together to create that effect. But there's unassuaged longing and nostalgia in here, interwoven with the horror, as well as an unflagging drive towards the final consummation. I still feel more for the story's characters, whether love or loathing, than for any others I've created to date. Tragedy, urban legend, Gothic romance, warped fairy tale of New York: it's all there. And of course, most important of all is the seductive allure of writing and of books – and what that can lead some people to do.

You may not like my answer to the mystery of the third book. But I hope you stay to find out."

*Paul StJohn Mackintosh*

"Paul StJohn Mackintosh is one of those writers who just seems to quietly get on with the business of producing great fiction... it's an excellent showcase for his obvious talents. His writing, his imagination, his ability to lay out a well-paced and intricate story in only 100 pages is a great testament to his skills."

—This is Horror

**blackshuckbooks.co.uk/signature**

Also from BLACK SHUCK *Signature*

# BLACK STAR, BLACK SUN

*by*

Rich Hawkins

"Black Star, Black Sun *is my tribute to Lovecraft, Ramsey Campbell, and the haunted fields of Somerset, where I seemed to spend much of my childhood. It's a story about going home and finding horror there when something beyond human understanding begins to invade our reality. It encompasses broken dreams, old memories, lost loved ones and a fundamentally hostile universe. It's the last song of a dying world before it falls to the Black Star."*

*Rich Hawkins*

———◆———

"Black Star, Black Sun *possesses a horror energy of sufficient intensity to make readers sit up straight. A descriptive force that shifts from the raw to the nuanced. A ferocious work of macabre imagination and one for readers of Conrad Williams and Gary McMahon."*

—Adam Nevill, author of *The Ritual*

"*Reading Hawkins' novella is like sitting in front of a guttering open fire. Its glimmerings captivate, hissing with irrepressible life, and then, just when you're most seduced by its warmth, it spits stinging embers your way. This is incendiary fiction. Read at arms' length."*

—Gary Fry, author of *Conjure House*

**blackshuckbooks.co.uk/signature**

# THE FINITE

*by*

## Kit Power

"The Finite *started as a dream; an image, really, on the edge of waking. My daughter and I, joining a stream of people walking past our house. We were marching together, and I saw that many of those behind us were sick, and struggling, and then I looked to the horizon and saw the mushroom cloud. I remember a wave of perfect horror and despair washing over me; the sure and certain knowledge that our march was doomed, as were we.*

*The image didn't make it into the story, but the feeling did. King instructs us to write about what scares us. In* The Finite, *I wrote about the worst thing I can imagine; my own childhood nightmare, resurrected and visited on my kid.*"

*Kit Power*

"The Finite *is* Where the Wind Blows *or* Threads *for the 21st century, played out on a tight scale by a father and his young daughter, which only serves to make it all the more heartbreaking.*"

—Priya Sharma, author of *Ormeshadow*

blackshuckbooks.co.uk/signature

# RICOCHET

*by*

# Tim Dry

"*With* Ricochet *I wanted to break away from the traditional linear form of storytelling in a novella and instead create a series of seemingly unrelated vignettes. Like the inconsistent chaos of vivid dreams I chose to create stand-alone episodes that vary from being fearful to blackly humorous to the downright bizarre. It's a book that you can dip into at any point but there is an underlying cadence that will carry you along, albeit in a strangely seductive new way.*

*Prepare to encounter a diverse collection of characters. Amongst them are gangsters, dead rock stars, psychics, comic strip heroes and villains, asylum inmates, UFOs, occult nazis, parisian ghosts, decaying and depraved royalty and topping the bill a special guest appearance by the Devil himself.*"

*Tim Dry*

---

*Reads like the exquisite lovechild of William Burroughs and Philip K. Dick's fiction, with some Ballard thrown in for good measure. Wonderfully imaginative, darkly satirical – this is a must read!*

—Paul Kane, author of *Sleeper(s)* and *Ghosts*

# ROTH-STEYR

*by*

## Simon Bestwick

"*You never know which ideas will stick in your mind, let alone where they'll go. *Roth-Steyr* began with an interest in the odd designs and names of early automatic pistols, and the decision to use one of them as a story title. What started out as an oddball short piece became a much longer and darker tale about how easily a familiar world can fall apart, how old convictions vanish or change, and why no one should want to live forever.*

*It's also about my obsession with history, in particular the chaotic upheavals that plagued the first half of the twentieth century and that are waking up again. Another 'long dark night of the European soul' feels very close today.*

*So here's the story of Valerie Varden. And her Roth-Steyr.*"

*Simon Bestwick*

———•———

"*A slice of pitch-black cosmic pulp, elegant and inventive in all the most emotionally engaging ways.*"

—Gemma Files, author of *In That Endlessness, Our End*

# A DIFFERENT KIND OF LIGHT

*by*

## Simon Bestwick

"When I first read about the Le Mans Disaster, over twenty years ago, I knew there was a story to tell about the newsreel footage of the aftermath – footage so appalling it was never released. A story about how many of us want to see things we aren't supposed to, even when we insist we don't.

What I didn't know was who would tell that story. Last year I finally realised: two lovers who weren't lovers, in a world that was falling apart. So at long last I wrote their story and followed them into a shadow land of old films, grief, obsession and things worse than death.

You only need open this book, and the film will start to play."

*Simon Bestwick*

———•———

"Compulsively readable, original and chilling. Simon Bestwick's witty, engaging tone effortlessly and brilliantly amplifies its edge-of-your-seat atmosphere of creeping dread. I'll be sleeping with the lights on."

—Sarah Lotz, author of *The Three, Day Four, The White Road* & *Missing Person*

# THE INCARNATIONS OF MARIELA PEÑA

*by*

## Steven J Dines

"The Incarnations of Mariela Peña *is unlike anything I have ever written. It started life (pardon the pun) as a zombie tale and very quickly became something else: a story about love and the fictions we tell ourselves.*

*During its writing, I felt the ghost of Charles Bukowski looking over my shoulder. I made the conscious decision to not censor either the characters or myself but to write freely and with brutal, sometimes uncomfortable, honesty. I was betrayed by someone I cared deeply for, and like Poet, I had to tell the story, or at least this incarnation of it. A story about how the past refuses to die.*"

*Steven J Dines*

———◆———

"*Call it literary horror, call it psychological horror, call it a journey into the darkness of the soul. It's all here. As intense and compelling a piece of work as I've read in many a year.*"

—Paul Finch, author of *Kiss of Death* and *Stolen*,
and editor of the *Terror Tales* series.

# THE DERELICT
## *by*
## Neil Williams

"The Derelict *is really a story of two derelicts – the events on the first and their part in the creation of the second.*

*With this story I've pretty much nailed my colours to the mast, so to speak. As the tale is intended as a tribute to stories by the likes of William Hope Hodgson or H P Lovecraft (with a passing nod to Coleridge's Ancient Mariner), where some terrible event is related in an unearthed journal or (as is the case here) by a narrator driven to near madness.*

*The primary influence on the story was the voyage of the Demeter, from Bram Stoker's* Dracula, *one of the more compelling episodes of that novel. Here the crew are irrevocably doomed from the moment they set sail. There is never any hope of escape or salvation once the nature of their cargo becomes apparent. This was to be my jumping off point with* The Derelict.

*Though I have charted a very different course from the one taken by Stoker, I have tried to remain resolutely true to the spirit of that genre of fiction and the time in which it was set."*

*Neil Williams*

———◆———

*"Fans of supernatural terror at sea will love* The Derelict. *I certainly did."*
—Stephen Laws, author of *Ferocity* and *Chasm*

**blackshuckbooks.co.uk/signature**

# AND THE NIGHT DID CLAIM THEM

*by*

## Duncan P Bradshaw

"*The night is a place where the places and people we see during the day are changed. Their properties – especially how we interact and consider them – are altered. But more than that, the night changes us as people. It's a time of day which both hides us away in the shadows and opens us up for reflection. Where we peer up at the stars, made aware of our utter insignificance and wonder, 'what if?' This book takes something that links every single one of us, and tries to illuminate its murky depths, finding things both familiar and alien. It's a story of loss, hope, and redemption; a barely audible whisper within, that even in our darkest hour, there is the promise of the light again.*"

*Duncan P Bradshaw*

"*A creepy, absorbing novella about loss, regret, and the blackness awaiting us all. Bleak as hell; dark and silky as a pint of Guinness - I loved it.*"

—James Everington, author of *Trying To Be So Quiet* and *The Quarantined City*

**blackshuckbooks.co.uk/signature**

# AZEMAN
## OR, THE TESTAMENT OF QUINCEY MORRIS

*by*

# Lisa Moore

"*How much do we really know about Quincey Morris?*

*In one of the greatest Grand-Guignol moments of all time, Dracula is caught feeding Mina blood from his own breast while her husband lies helpless on the same bed. In the chaos that follows, Morris runs outside, ostensibly in pursuit. "I could see Quincey Morris run across the lawn," Dr. Seward says, "and hide himself in the shadow of a great yew-tree. It puzzled me to think why he was doing this..." Then the doctor is distracted, and we never do find out.*

*This story rose up from that one question: Why, in this calamitous moment, did the brave and stalwart Quincey Morris hide behind a tree?*"

*Lisa Moore*

———•———

"*A fresh new take on one of the many enigmas of Dracula – just what is Quincey Morris's story?*"

—Kim Newman, author of the *Anno Dracula* series

# SHADE OF STILLTHORPE
*by*
## Tim Major

"It's fair to say that parenthood has dominated my thoughts – and certainly my identity – for the last nine years. While I love my children unconditionally, I'm morbidly fascinated by the idea of parenthood lacking an instinctive bond to counter the difficulties and sacrifices of such a period of life. And I'm afraid of any possible future in which that bond might be weaker.

Identity is a slippery thing. More than anything, I'm scared of losing it – my own, and those of the people I love. Several of my novels and stories have related to this fear. In Shade of Stillthorpe, it's quite literal: how would you react if your child was unrecognisable, suddenly, in all respects?"

*Tim Major*

———◆———

*A seemingly impossible premise becomes increasingly real in this inventive and heartbreaking tale of loss."*

—Lucie McKnight Hardy, author of *Dead Relatives*

"Parenthood is a forest of emotions, including jealousy, confusion and terror, in Shade of Stillthorpe. It's a dark mystery that resonated deeply with me."
—Aliya Whiteley, author of *The Loosening Skin*

# SORROWMOUTH

*by*

## Simon Avery

"*For a long time Sorrowmouth existed as three or four separate ideas in different notebooks until one day, in a flash of divine inspiration, I recognised the common ground they shared with each other. A man trekking from one roadside memorial to another, in pursuit of grief; Beachy Head and its long dark history of suicide; William Blake and his angelic visions on Peckham Rye; Blake again with The Ghost of a Flea; a monstrous companion, bound by lifes' cruelty...*

*As I wrote I discovered these disparate elements were really about me getting to some deeper truth about myself, and about all the people I've known in my life, about the struggles we all have that no one save for loved ones see – alcoholism, dependence, self doubt, grief, mental illness. Sorrowmouth is about the mystery hiding at the heart of all things, making connections in the depths of sorrow, and what you have to sacrifice for a moment of vertigo.*"

*Simon Avery*

———•———

"*Sorrowmouth is a story for these dark days. Simon Avery summons the spirit of William Blake in this visionary exploration of the manifestations of our grief and pain.*"

—Priya Sharma, author of *Ormeshadow*

# THE DREAD
# THEY LEFT BEHIND

*by*

## Gary Fry

"*The seed of this novella was a single image I'd long had in mind before composition. A young boy standing in a farmyard no longer knowing which hand he led with. That struck me as a promising metaphor for something my conscious mind had yet to catch up with, and indeed it was another few years before I finally figured it all out. By this time I'd returned to my early love of the classic dark novella. Lovecraft, obviously, but also a renewed appreciation of Arthur Machen, particularly his criminally underrated 'The Terror'. In that piece, I was struck by its accumulative, almost investigative structure, the way it drew upon different sources of information to conjure a vision packed with verisimilitude.*

*In* The Dread They Left Behind, *I wanted to evoke an isolated rural community via the medium of a retrospective first-person narrator along the lines of he who regales us in HPL's 'The Color out of Space'. The difference is that mine is directly exposed to and physically affected by the historical events. Along with all the requisite intrigue and frights, the piece allowed me to explore concerns I have about political extremism. It took a long while to get right -- I tinkered with it for years. But for me it embodies everything I hold dear in the field. Whether it does so successfully, I leave for readers to determine.*"

*Gary Fry*